*Planetary blockades. Rampant viral outbreaks. Can two ex-lovers forge a path through the stars to save their world?*

*Independent trader Gavril Danilovich is slowly slipping into madness. Stuck in quarantine on a dying planet, his raw talent to feel everyone's emotions has him wrestling with waves of terror and rage. So when the woman who holds his heart offers an opportunity for isolation by repairing a mothballed freighter, he jumps at the chance.*

*Anitra Helden can't outrun her past. Hiring the only man she trusts to fix up a spaceship destined to fill a new settlement with supplies, she fears for the population's safety when thieves steal valuable goods. And after she's invited to join a covert plan to protect all colonists, she's terrified one misspoken word could burn all her bridges.*

*Racing the clock to prepare the vessel in time, Gavril struggles to master his painful empathy or face being trapped on the ground forever. And with the stranded citizens desperate for Anitra's help, she's confronted with the decision to expose her dangerous history... or lose everything she's built.*

*Can they escape the stricken planet before they're doomed by intergalactic corruption?*

# ALSO BY CAROL VAN NATTA

**Central Galactic Concordance Space Opera Series**

- Last Ship Off Polaris-G (Novella)
- Overload Flux (Book 1)
- Minder Rising (Book 2)
- Zero Flux (Novella)
- Pico's Crush (Book 3)
- Pet Trade (Novella)
- Jumper's Hope (Book 4)
- Cats of War (Novella)
- Galactic Search and Rescue (Novella)
- Escape from Nova Nine (Novella)
- Spark Transform (Book 5)

**Paranormal Romance**

- Shifter Mate Magic (Ice Age Shifters #1)
- Shift of Destiny (Ice Age Shifters #2)
- Heart of a Dire Wolf (Ice Age Shifters #3)
- Dire Wolf Wanted (Ice Age Shifters #4)
- Shifter's Storm (Ice Age Shifters #5)
- In Graves Below (Magic, NM)

**Retro Science Fiction Comedy**

- Hooray for Holopticon

# LAST SHIP OFF POLARIS-G

## A CENTRAL GALACTIC CONCORDANCE NOVELLA

### CAROL VAN NATTA

CHAVANCH PRESS

# 1

* Frontier Planet Polaris-Gamma * GDAT 3233.012 *

Supply Depot Manager Anitra Helden counted her lucky stars that she'd stumbled across an abandoned interstellar freighter. She hoped Trader Gavril Danilovich's evaluation would bring rare good news in a year of bad, worse, and catastrophic events. Funnily enough, she trusted him more than anyone local she'd known and worked with for the last three years. Nothing like a slow-moving apocalypse to bring out the worst in everyone.

In the final months of life on the formerly up-and-coming frontier planet of Polaris-Gamma, the settlers had become reckless, volatile, and mean. The settlement company that had organized the planet's colonization had gotten greedy. The government's overworked and understaffed planetary law enforcement barely kept the pot from boiling over. And between broad-daylight thefts, city infrastructure failures, and near-nightly riots, Aetheres city enforcers were at burnout.

Dust made clouds in the chilled air, creating a golden haze in the shafts of autumn sunlight that streamed in from the cavernous airdome's open skylights. The mottled surface of the massive old freighter looked like a canvas painting. Anitra had traveled in hundreds of interstellar ships, large and small, but never stood on the top of one in a repair dock. Below her boots spanned a hundred and twenty meters by ninety meters of transit space-etched incalloy. Her mind balked at trying to imagine its true size, even if she could see it.

Gavril had every reason to tell Pol-G's government to suck a hot flux hose. A month ago, Pol-G's government-run spaceport had impounded his cargo and sealed off his interstellar trader ship—his sole means of livelihood—on a dubious charge of unpaid landing fees from a previous visit. He'd been losing customers every galactic standard day since then. He was only with her now, well outside the city in the defunct ship repair hangar, because they had a history.

Well, more like a chance meeting two years ago that had led to a long weekend together that became a glorious long week. Unfortunately, fantastic sex and dreams of different star lanes were no match for his scheduled trading commitments throughout the galaxy. Or for her ground-based responsibilities as a newly promoted government supply depot manager, a job she'd worked hard to get. Besides, returning to any of the Central Galactic Concordance's five-hundred-plus member planets wasn't an option for her. They were both well past the age when a chance for love made anything seem possible. She hadn't known he'd gotten stuck on Pol-G until she'd run into him again two weeks ago in the same pub where she'd first met him.

He wore his life experience well, she thought. Body shops could make anyone look any age they wanted, from seventeen to one hundred seventy. However, as far as she knew, Gavril only went in for regular checkups and maintenance, so he'd won the genetics lottery. She knew him to be fifty-six, but he looked at least fifteen years younger. He delighted in whimsical hair and eye colors, and artistic skin decoration.

She didn't look her own age of fifty-five, either, but that was thanks to a full body makeover that made her look early thirties and of deliberately vague Afro-Euro heritage. She didn't expect to see another body shop for multiple decades, owing to circumstances that had forced her to set fire to her former career in the Central Galactic Concordance and flee to the sanctuary of the frontier. She'd set down roots on Pol-G, hoping to age gracefully there for the next hundred years, far away from the CGC and out of reach of the Citizen Protection Service. And look how well *that* had turned out.

She sealed the collar of her green half-cloak against the chill of the disused hangar and walked briskly back to the stairway up to the banks of computers and large-format displays where Gavril worked. She wouldn't even have recognized them as comps, much less that they controlled the repair dock's cameras, scanners, and probes below, if Gavril hadn't told her. She'd found a plausible excuse to get the dock's power turned on and neighborhood batteries recharged without mentioning the existence of the dormant freighter in the underground repair silo. Good thing she'd remembered Gavril trained as a ship engineer and worked in a commercial shipyard for twenty years before taking up the life of an independent trader. And good thing he also liked tinkering with old ships, because the *Deset Diamantov* was at least ninety years old.

She stood to the side, out of his way, surreptitiously admiring the view. His imposing nose and generous mouth looked European, but the shape of his eyes and cheekbones, and his wiry strength, spoke of Asian heritage. His currently long black-, blue-, and gold-beaded braids hid the pilot's skulljack behind his bejeweled ear. It made an intriguingly handsome combination, and was one of the qualities that had first attracted her to him. He was sexy as hell. His grumpy, sarcastic surface hid a generous nature and a lively sense of the absurd that made her laugh.

She didn't need her empath talent to tell that he was enjoying himself now, but she dropped her shield and let herself be soothed by the uncontained flavors of it anyway. Not exactly ethical, but she needed it. They'd be back in the sulking, raging city soon enough.

He slid his hands into his jacket pockets and turned to her. "That's the final system check." The corner of his mouth twitched with humor. "Tell me again how the planetary government *lost* a freighter the size of a gravball stadium."

She laughed at the acerbity in his tone. "I don't think they ever knew they had it. After our first visit, I did some digging. When the settlement company's illegal embargo depressed off-planet trade last year, the shipyard owners emptied their financial accounts and left in a hurry. Their major investor went bankrupt a month later. Pol-G eventually confiscated the property for taxes owed and sent the city an audit request, but it never happened, probably because it was on a list of hundreds. Aetheres lost half its population and businesses in the six months before the blockade. Oh, sorry, the 'pandemic quarantine for the safety of the Concordance.'" She made air quotes with her fingers. "I only found this place because it's tagged in my office's records as a suspended transportation warehouse—probably a translation error —and I was hoping it had a missing government cache of pre-blight mealpacks. When I read the actual business name on the hangar doors, I thought of you." If she was honest, she'd thought of him a lot since running into him in the pub, and remembered how they'd synced so well. She'd put off contacting him again, because the timing tanked and her job kept her insanely busy, but this was too good an opportunity to pass up.

Her growly stomach wanted the lunch she'd left in the flitter they'd parked just inside the gigantic front doors, but she wanted to hear Gavril's evaluation more.

"Who owned the ship?" His Standard English held the flavor of a Slavic accent with certain words.

She shook her head. "No record. Best guess, the shipyard was holding it hostage until the owner paid the repair bill." She tilted her head toward the diagnostic displays. "Maybe the shipcomps know?"

"No, they're flatlined." A three-tone chime sounded from the console, loud enough to echo against the high walls. He turned and manipulated the holo interface. Data streamed on one of the displays, then went blank. He shut down the console and made a face as he pressed a control that retracted the displays. "It's good news, bad news."

"Bad first." Better to know what she was up against, rather than living on hope.

"Absolute zero fuel, either system or flux. Two out of four coils in the system drive are fried, along with the gravity compensators, atmosphere wing controls, and thrusters. All the comps are flatlined—engine, nav, enviro, security, comms, everything. No working escape pods. No weapons, not even amped-up debris lasers. The incalloy is too thin where the ship took heavy energy weapon damage. Someone sealed off the largest loading airlock rather than replace it." He shook his head in disgust. "The cargo holds are a catastrophe waiting to happen—a jumble of mismatched shipping crates bolted onto a random spider web of cross-struts."

"No wonder they abandoned it." She sighed. "What's the good news?"

"It's a good design, with good bones. The interstellar drive is only ten years old and sized correctly for the ship and a full cargo. That would have been a deal-killer. Everything else is fixable, right here"—he circled a finger to indicate the hangar and everything below it—"if you can line up shipbuilders, engineers, data techs, materials, replacement parts, incalloy, and someone to redesign and refit the cargo holds. And an ocean-sized tanker or two of fuel."

She had a lot to think about, and as usual, too little

time. "Let's close up here and talk about it in the flitter." She shivered. "The *warm* flitter."

SHE TOOK OFF, then released control of the flitter's flight to the city's traffic control system. Reaching into the insulated bag she'd brought, she pulled two still-warm meat pies out and handed him one.

He gave her a quick smile as he unwrapped it and took a bite. "You made this? It's good."

"Thanks." She took her own first bite. "I like cooking, when I can."

"So do I." His mild words didn't match the uncontained flare of annoyance from him, probably because he'd lost access to his kitchen when the spaceport sealed his ship. She raised her shields so her own mixed emotions wouldn't add to his stress.

She finished her pie quickly, then handed him a pouch of filtered water and took one for herself.

"I wish I had the time to be delicate about this, but I don't. First, while my title is still supply depot manager, my new unofficial job is supply logistics for a mass lift-off from the planet. I'm not high enough in the food chain to know when, or where any of us are going, but it's coming. I'm sure you've heard the rumors everywhere. Second, the government commandeered *all* ships, not just yours, and is conscripting anyone with a pilot or navigation certificate, even if it's thirty years out of date. If you agree to pilot your ship and pass a screening, they'll clear the lien on it once you get to whatever refuge they're sending your passengers to." She shrugged. "That's the official line, at any rate."

She took a sip of water to give herself a moment to organize her thoughts. "If we can get the *Diamantov* operational again, I want to fill it with everything of value I can get my hands on to trade or sell, so our people don't show up on someone else's proverbial doorstep empty-handed. I think I can find everything needed to fix the ship, but I need someone I trust to take charge of the refit and do it right." She looked him straight in the eye. "That's you."

As she would have expected from a professional trader, neither his face nor body language gave anything away. She resisted the temptation to drop her shields and activate her empath talent to see what his uncontained emotions could tell her.

"Would this master-level, supervisory buildmaster gig be for the Pol-G government that commandeered my ship, even though I might have agreed to help if they'd asked? Or for you?"

"Both, I guess. The government can't pay CGC hard credit because the settlement company would just garnish it, but I can arrange that they pay in interstellar flux fuel and an energy recharge for your ship. Flux is the one thing Pol-G has in abundance—arguably what got us into this mess in the first place. I can offer two things in trade." She held up one finger. "First, I'll do my damnedest to get your ship released so you can stay or go as you please, though you'd still have to be screened." She added another finger. "Second, I'll train you how to use and contain your minder empath talent, so you can handle being in crowds, or stand being around emotional people who are broadcasting so loud they make your ears bleed."

He turned away to look out the side window. She'd given him a lot to think about, so she unfolded her tablet and busied herself with her exponentially growing task list, to give him the gift of silence.

When he finally spoke, it wasn't the question she expected.

"How long have you known about my minder talent?" His flat tone matched his expressionless face.

"Since that last day together. I wasn't looking for it, and you don't use it often. I'm a multi-talent minder—empath, shielder..." She pointed to her temple. "I'm trained to always stay shielded, even when I sleep, so I didn't feel your talent flare until we had that last, ah, disagreement."

He snorted. "The one where I told you I was leaving with or without you, and you told me to suck flux?"

She really needed to find some new insults. "Yeah, that one. I couldn't have come with you then, and you knew it, but I could have been more diplomatic."

He hunched one shoulder and looked away. "I pushed too hard."

"I think your empath talent is high level. Sifters are better at sensing minder talents than mid-level shielders like me, so I could be wrong, but didn't CPS testing catch it?" One of the Citizen Protection Service's more benign missions was to test every child in the Central Galactic Concordance for minder talents at ages twelve and seventeen. Maybe a quarter of those tested positive for talents. Useful high-level talents usually brought scholarships to the prestigious CPS Academy and Institute, plus bonus payments to the family. Not many parents turned down the prestige or the opportunity. Hers certainly hadn't.

He looked straight ahead at the approaching city skyline. "My mother didn't believe in talent testing, because of my father. She faked my records." He shook his head. "Probably wouldn't have found anything, anyway. It didn't show up until I was in my early twenties."

She wanted to follow that intriguing trail, because she knew very little of his past, but couldn't afford the distraction. She also couldn't afford certain questions about her own background. "I'm CPS Institute-educated, and have trained a lot of minders in the field. Even if you turn down the *Diamantov* deal, I'd be willing to teach you. My empath talent developed first, so I know what it's like not to be able to shut the world out." She darted a look at him and took a guess. "Especially if you don't understand what's happening."

He glanced at her, startled, then looked away again. "I thought I was going insane."

"Oh, yeah. Kids who tell the wrong person get called liars or attention-seekers." She gave him a wry smile. "Testing is good for telling young minders they aren't crazy, but being a known minder doesn't exactly make you welcome in polite society. Then there's the whole 'all minders are cheaters' thing. The registration law finally died twenty years ago, so it's getting better, but I can't blame your mother for not wanting the life of a minder for her son."

They passed over a sprawling tract of a never-completed commercial and residential community. From the air, it looked like it would have been a pleasant place to live.

"What's the screening you mentioned?"

She gave him an apologetic look. "It's a telepathic scan. No one trusts RSI—that's the settlement company —not to use spies against us. All it would take is one torp headed for the military blockade, and they'd make a ring around the planet with the remains of our refugee ships."

"Let me guess. If I refuse the scan, they keep my ship." His lips thinned and his eyes narrowed. "That's just farking fabulous."

"If it helps to know, the telepath already scanned me, and he's good at his job. So far, he's kept everyone's secrets." Including a couple of her own that could get her killed if revealed.

She checked the console, to make sure the flitter was still being controlled by the increasingly glitchy traffic control system. TCS maintenance didn't have as high a priority as keeping the peace long enough to get the hell off a dying planet.

Below them, the bleached skeletons of once lushly green trees made it look like winter, even though it was barely the first days of autumn. A year ago, a virulent fungus had arrived in a seemingly innocent shipment of fuel-crop planting seeds. Funny how the pale, powdery blight affected multiple phyla of plant life and mutated faster than the bioengineers could tailor antifungals to kill it. Even funnier how it had arrived exactly thirty days after the Pol-G government refused to honor a CGC court order to pay the settlement company a huge penalty for early settlement debt payoff.

Settlement companies invested heavily in terraforming suitable planets and marketed them to frontier settlers willing to pay, expecting to reap nearly a century of interest payments, while also selling overpriced services to the settlers. Pol-G's decades-early debt payoff pissed off the settlement company to no end.

Debates raged as to whether the company knew the blight would destroy the whole planet's terraformed ecology, or if the company had been as unpleasantly surprised as the settlers when the royal ratfucking backfired. Either way, it wasn't getting its penalty money now.

She shook off her melancholy. It wasn't helping get anything done. The countdown clock on the console said the flitter would reach her supply depot's airpad in twelve minutes. She folded her tablet and turned her seat so it was easier to look at Gavril.

He turned his seat to face her. "Could you use your talent to make me want to say yes?"

"Maybe." She tilted her head. "Do you want me to? So you can blame me if things go chaotic?" She smiled wryly. "Which they probably will, because that's just how we glide here on the happiest planet in the galaxy."

"No, I wanted to know if you were influencing me, because I'm inclined to agree to your insane project, and it's not like me." He blew out a noisy breath. "I don't like people."

"Thank you." She couldn't keep the smile off her face. "You'll probably be cursing my name hourly for the foreseeable future, but please know I'm grateful." She hadn't expected he'd sign on for her half-baked plan, so now she had to follow through. "Do you have time this afternoon to make a prioritized list of what you'll need, with alternates and options?"

He snorted. "I'll clear my calendar."

She thought about giving him one of the empty offices in the supply depot, but the less anyone knew about the freighter and what she was planning to do with it, the better. She liked most of her employees, but didn't know if they could keep a secret as big as the *Diamantov*.

"Where are you staying?" She pulled out her tablet again. "Here's what I'm thinking. I'd like to have you move to the repair dock, far away from prying eyes. Maybe on the ship? You'll need a vehicle, too. The city is overloaded with repossessed and abandoned flitters and haulers. I think I can work a deal to store some of their overflow at my new remote transportation warehouse."

Gavril leaned forward. "I'll move to the dock this afternoon if you'll let me. Even if I have to sleep in a tent, eat mealpacks, and urinate in the woods." A bleak expression crossed his face. "You should know that the city is making me crazy. I've had to chem myself nightly to get any sleep."

She looked up from her list and gave him an assessing look. "Can you quit the chems on your own?"

He nodded. "Yes. I don't like them, but I can't handle crowds." He pointed a thumb toward the back. "A huge, empty ship will be paradise."

She wouldn't find a buildmaster she trusted in time,

and she wanted to trust Gavril. "It won't be entirely empty, if I can get you some help."

He waved a hand in dismissal. "A few people are no problem. I'll add specialty skills to the list."

"Good." She smiled, basking in the all-too-rare sense of hope, before it got crushed again. "You're a lifesaver."

## 2

* Polaris-Gamma * GDAT 3233.015 *

Gavril hunched in his seat against the misery and despair of two hundred people that beat at his uncontrolled empathic talent. His head hurt already, and he'd only been in the Pol-G tax authority's crowded waiting area for ten minutes. He couldn't tell who was waiting for a regular audit arbiter and who was waiting for the secret telepathic screening, but no one was happy to be there.

The only exception was Anitra, seated next to him, diligently working on her tablet and subvocalizing into the earwire adhered to her jaw and tucked into her right ear. She was a cool oasis of no emotions at all, thanks to her shielder talent. In the two lessons they'd had time for in the last three days, she'd taught him to recognize the difference between an active shield and simple containment. He wasn't bad at containing his own emotions when needed, but blocking others by shutting down his talent remained elusive. He didn't want to think about influencing the emotions of others, and couldn't imagine doing it for multiple hundreds for crowd control, the way she claimed trained high-level empaths could.

He straightened up in the uncomfortable seat and told himself to quit grousing. After nearly a month of sitting on his ass in a rundown hostel in a shady neighborhood and watching his trader business and the planet's prime city fall apart around him, even chemming himself insensible had gotten boring. The city's joy houses had too many achingly lonely people using sex for solace. Besides, prices for everything had gone stratospheric, and he'd rather pay for food, or even a good massage to relieve the chronic tension in his neck and shoulders.

Serving as buildmaster for refitting the *Diamantov* kept him busy and gave him a remote refuge from the crowds. It was a relief to only have to interact with four other people so far, though Anitra's efforts would soon bring more.

He cast a sidelong glance at her. During their vacation-week affair two years ago, he'd synced with her sense of adventure and enjoyed her zest for life. She was also nova-hot sexy and felt right in his arms. They'd lived in the moment, with no regard for the past or thought to the future, and paid the price for it in the end when reality smacked them both upside the head.

He still saw flashes of that happier woman, especially when she teased him, but she was eating, sleeping, and breathing her job, with one eye on her tablet and the other on the clock. She presented a picture-perfect image of a harried, mid-level bureaucrat, with her conservative corporate suits, unadorned light brown skin, and always-up dark brown hair. They effectively camouflaged her creative, agile mind and her determination.

She probably had the most accurate set of physical asset records in the government, owing to her patient diligence in hunting them down, and she used them to her advantage. The old ground haulers, aircars, and flitters she sent to be stored at the repair dock just happened to be loaded with ship-building supplies, or just happened to be driven or flown by an unemployed metals tech, or an engineer who used to work for the repair dock, or a skilled navigator who could help get the shipcomps online.

A huge display took up half of one wall of the tax office, illustrating the tangle of corridors and offices, and the waiting queues for each. Visitors stopped at the front kiosk to enter their request and pick up an electronic token for their place in line. The buzz of quiet conversation ebbed and flowed. He woke the percomp on his wrist to read something other than depressing newstrends about more animal extinctions, riots, and failed blockade runs, but the increasing pressure in his head interfered with his concentration. He rubbed his temples.

A hushed conversation behind him caught his attention.

"...that's the sixth runner this week," a man's voice whispered.

"Good. The more flatliners get themselves arrested at the blockade means more for the people who stay." A woman's voice, more hissed than whispered. She was a tangle of fear and anger.

"The slaggin' government can't even keep the planet network up, or we could do this all online and not waste an evening here. What makes you think they'll do any better with power or water?" Despair colored the man's tone.

"I'll drill a well and put up solar collectors for the grow houses. Better than being blasted out of orbit, or giving up the land I spent my life's savings on. Frelling blight can't last forever."

The wall display blinked and chimed to indicate an update. A chorus of grumbling and groans arose when the countdown clocks added another thirty minutes to the average wait time. Several people stood and made their way to office various doors, holding their blinking tokens like winning lottery tickets. The waves of emotion crashed into his head with his every heartbeat.

A message from Anitra pinged on his percomp. They'd already set up a closed-system secure channel to keep their comms private.

*A: You're hurting. I can shield you, but it'll feel like you're suddenly deaf.*

Gavril looked at her with his peripheral vision, but couldn't read anything in her expression as she continued to commune with her tablet. He tapped his earwire and subvocalized his reply.

*G: Yes, please. I'll cope. I'll trade you for a massage later.*

He'd trained as a physical therapist, before his untamed empath talent made it too uncomfortable, and he was still good with his hands, or so Anitra had said two years ago. Her fingers on the tablet slowed. Suddenly, he was alone in his head, and feeling like fog muffled all his physical senses. Intellectually, he knew that his ears still heard the sounds of voices and coughing, and his nose still smelled the mixture of ash and sweat in the room, but it all felt weirdly muted, like an experience holo in his trader ship's tiny immersion room. As much as he'd assumed he ignored his despised talent, he obviously depended on it far more than he realized.

*G: Feels weird, like you said. Does it hurt you?*

*A: No. If you don't fight me, I can do this for hours. I can't feel others while I'm shielding you.*

*G: Problem?*

Out of the corner of his eye, he saw her shrug, as if to say that everything had tradeoffs.

He took the opportunity to look at the people around him, for once without the distraction of trying not to feel them. Some looked beaten down, some looked defiant, but they all looked like they expected another shoe to drop in a room already full of them. He'd seen a smaller microcosm of it every night in the pub, before he'd started chemming himself to sleep to keep his sanity.

His percomp pinged another message from Anitra.

*A: Blond man in red, the row near the east door, three seats down. Know him? See his pilot cert. Sixty years of commercial shipping experience.*

Gavril stood and stretched, twisting his body so he could see the man's face in the reflection of the glass doors. He sat again and read through the list of freighters the man's cert listed.

*G: Don't recognize him, but I know some of the ship types he piloted. He'd be good, if he's not a jerk.*

He saw her smile as she got his reply.

*A: If pilots' certs listed attitude, they'd never get work.*

*G: Good thing I work for myself.*

The wall display changed again, tokens lit up, and random people throughout the hall stood moments later. The east and north doors opened to disgorge a few people. The man in red stood and headed toward the north.

Gavril twitched when the token in his hand lit up and vibrated. The readout told him to proceed to the north door labeled "Delta" and follow the blue lighting path. Anitra was already folding her tablet and stuffing it in the inside pocket of her jacket-cloak. He'd been ambivalent about her posing as his tax advisor so she could introduce him to Dammerk, the scanning telepath, but now he was grateful for her support. And for her shield, because it gave him time to shore up his defenses and become the cool-headed trader, taking in everything and giving away nothing.

The wide hallways allowed them to walk side by side. When he hesitated at an intersection, waiting for the corridor lighting to tell him which way to go, Anitra caught his eye and tapped her temple. He took it as her warning she was dropping the shield. The fog around his senses lifted as the chaser lights told them to turn right. He could again feel the concentrated presence of all the people in the lobby, but distance and thick walls made it easier to tolerate.

After a few meters, the corridor turned right again, to

reveal a closed double doorway about twelve meters down at the end, all executive-gray glass with an iridescent government emblem. He and Anitra both hesitated when they saw the man in red already there, holding his token up to the wall comp.

The doors slid open. Shouting erupted from the room. Fear and rage blasted through Gavril's head like an explosion. He instinctively wrapped his arms around Anitra and pivoted her back around the corner. Beamer fire whined. A man's voice cried out in pain.

Anitra's feet tangled with his, sending them bouncing off the wall as high-pitched stunner fire echoed.

The pressure of emotion faded to nothing.

Silence.

Anitra steadied herself using his shoulder. Her face was pale and grim. "Three people..." Her expression suddenly twisted in pain, and her knees buckled. He caught and held her upright as she sagged against him.

"We're leaving." He slid his arm around her waist and urged her to walk.

She stumbled along with him a couple of steps, wincing in pain, then straightened and stopped. "We have to go back."

"Bad idea, unless you're wearing flexin armor underwear."

"Everyone's dead." She rubbed her temple. "That was Dammerk's last blast. I was the closest mind he recognized, and my shields were down. He was top-level, so he'd have blown past them anyway." She pulled away from him. "I have to get his percomp."

Every interstellar trader knew never to get involved in

local trouble, but he couldn't let her go alone. "Fast, then."

She nodded and pushed off into a half-run. He pulled his shockstick out of his cargo pants pocket and thumbed it on as he caught up with her. It wasn't a lethal weapon like a beamer, but it was handy in a scuffle.

The man in red lay like a broken doll on the floor, with a charred hole in his chest. The glass doors kept trying to close, bouncing against his legs.

Gavril held his blinking token to the wallcomp, and the doors stayed open.

Anitra took a deep breath, then clenched her jaw tight and entered the gilded executive office. He followed, but stayed in the doorway to keep it open. The carnage took him by surprise.

A beefy, fashionably blue-skinned, bald man lay in a heap just inside the door, a high-powered stunner still in his hand. A painfully thin, white-skinned man with a bruised and bloody face slumped sideways in the wingback chair behind a clear glass desk. Blood dripped from his empty hand onto a small hand beamer on the floor. Behind the chair, three more sets of legs were visible, where more bodies had been shoved against the wall.

Gavril took a shallow breath, trying not to take in more of the smell of blood and voided fluids than he had to. "Shit."

Anitra stepped around the desk and gingerly lifted the lapel of the white-skinned man's blood-covered, maroon-striped jacket. Her hand shook as she unclasped the necklace-style percomp and pulled it off the body.

Gavril caught her eye and pointed to the growing wet spot in the carpet, so she wouldn't step in it. She skirted it and walked determinedly past him out into the corridor. He pocketed his shockstick as they walked away.

They went quickly past several closed doors and the corridor turn. At the next hallway intersection, their luck ran out when a security guard walked by, slowing as she took a second lingering glance at Anitra's gray, sweaty face.

"Fresher?" asked Gavril, taking hold of Anitra's elbow. "My wife is sick."

The guard pointed behind her. "On the left, beyond the water station."

Gavril hustled Anitra down the hall and shoved the fresher door open, then sealed it behind them. She staggered to the counter and took several deep, gulping breaths. "I fucking hate blood."

He crossed to the sink and wetted a couple of towels to hand to her. "The guard will remember us."

She wiped her hands and face, then stuffed the now pink-tinged towels into her jacket pocket. "Yeah." She took another deep breath and pulled out the percomp she'd lifted off the dead man. "Dammerk's last request was that I use this to ping a message to Kareem Ferrsi."

"The head of Planetary Law Enforcement?" He was on the nightly newstrends a lot, usually offering patient, measured responses to inflammatory accusations by burn-the-blight activists or delusional appeasement ideas from politicians.

She nodded as she entered a key to open the interface, then quickly synced the percomp to her earwire. She tagged an icon in the holo display, then began subvocalizing.

He suppressed a frown. So much for staying uninvolved. He moved back to the door and deliberately activated his empath talent as best he could, trying to get a sense of where people were in relation to the fresher. The crowded lobby was like a writhing ball of plasma strings, but he could feel smaller, closer, more distinct thread tangles that roughly corresponded to the offices they'd walked by. No one had found the bloody executive office yet, or he'd have felt their shock.

Anitra started to close the percomp interface, but jerked when it vibrated with an incoming ping. She read it rapidly and answered via subvocalization.

He tuned it out and went back to using his ears and his talent to watch their backs. She'd been straight and honest with him so far, which was more than he could say of anyone else on the planet. He trusted she'd tell him what the frelling hell was going on soon enough.

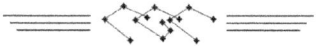

GAVRIL TURNED his back to the breeze and looked up at the midnight sky, wishing for stars. The sky over Aetheres was never clear because of the constant debris from dying trees, ash from a continent's worth of burned crops, and the ever-present wind. The city lights reflected off the pale dust, giving it a claustrophobic feel, as if a city that had once boasted a growing population of three hundred thousand was being wrapped in soft cotton batting for storage.

Still, the corner balcony of Anitra's twentieth-floor apartment offered a spectacular night-time view of the glittering city. The door slid open behind him. "Come get food and news, before I crater."

He stepped in and slid the door closed behind him. The rich smell of stew made his mouth water as he sat at the place she'd set for him at the kitchen bar.

She ladled stew into two bowls, then pushed one to him. "Mostly premade, except the extra onions and mushrooms."

"Better than I've had in weeks." He smiled.

They ate quietly and quickly. Even though exhaustion rounded her shoulders and hollowed her eyes, she was still as intriguingly vibrant as he remembered. Not vapidly pretty, but with subtle beauty that snuck up on people.

He found himself wanting to hold her, to take care of her. Now that he'd seen her operating so effectively in her professional environment, and the homey comfort of her apartment full of professional-quality art she'd painted herself, he began to understand why his offer of traveling the galaxy had held little appeal.

She finished her stew and put their empty bowls in the sanitizer, then leaned against the counter, cradling a glass of red wine.

"Here's what I know. The blue-skinned dead man was a mercenary pilot and aspiring spy named Rausch. He was a low-level telepath and a ramper who thought he could fool Dammers. When Dammerk blew past Rausch's containment, Rausch ramped up to lightning speed and shot Dammerk with a stunner. In case you didn't know, by the way, stunners usually disrupt minder talents, sometimes for hours."

He twitched a smile. "I'll add it to my list of things not to get shot with."

"Rausch belonged to a group that thinks if we leave, the military will do to Pol-G what they did to Rashad Tarana and poison the planet for all time. Since Rausch's cover was blown, he took the opportunity to do damage. He tied Dammerk to the chair, killed each of the pilots as they came in, then waited for the queue system to send the next. Dammerk recovered from the stunner sooner than Rausch expected and shot Rausch with the hand beamer, but one of his shots went wide and killed the man in red that we saw. Rausch's last act was to stun Dammerk multiple times." She took a sip of wine. "Shouldn't have been fatal, except Dammerk was already very sick from enhancement-drug withdrawal. He was also a top-level telepath, which is why he was able to hit me with that big mental package even as he was dying." She rubbed her temple. "He wasn't exactly an organized thinker. I'm still trying to sort it out in my head. I briefed Ferrsi on what I could."

Gavril had no experience with telepaths, that he knew of. Anitra's description made him want to avoid them in the future. "What happened after Ferrsi sent me away?" She'd hastily given him the location ref and access codes to her apartment, since they didn't want a public transportation record of him going back to the repair dock.

She rolled her eyes. "I got *promoted*."

He gave her a sympathetic smile. "An honor you could do without?"

"Good and bad, I guess. I like making sure things are done right, but I'm overwhelmed as it is." She swirled her wine and watched it a moment. "After Dammerk scanned me a couple of months ago, he recommended me for the committee. They didn't want to add more members back then, but now that Dammerk is gone, I'm in. Ferrsi took me to an emergency meeting right after, which is why it's so frickin' late. From what the committee told me, the plan is either audacious as hell or warped beyond all recognition, depending on how you look at it." She took a large gulp of her wine.

He started to ask for details, then stopped himself. Secrets and hidden agendas irked him, but realistically, he was a public display wall compared to Anitra, with her useful shielder talent. If he didn't know anything, he couldn't it give away.

"Here's the part that concerns you. I told them my idea about the freighter. The top minister of my government department is a man named Dalgono, and he's on the committee. He supported my project, provided we find a suitable pilot and spacer crew. I got the committee to release your ship—you should get the notice tomorrow. I told them you're my massage therapist and I trust you. I didn't tell them you're the supervising refit engineer for the *Diamantov* because I'm greedy. I don't want any politicians stealing you for themselves or their rich donors." She gave him a sardonic smile. "I vouched for you, so you better not turn out to be a settlement company spy."

He shook his head. "Not me. I hate working for anyone else." He twitched an eyebrow. "Present boss excepted."

"Thanks. Ferrsi convinced the committee that only I should know where the *Diamantov* is for now, in keeping with their policy for compartmentalizing knowledge. The others didn't mind, probably because they think it's a long shot." She gave him a lopsided smile. "I may have implied the ship is small and in terrible shape."

He chuckled. "Always better to under-promise and over-deliver."

"Exactly." She held up her wine glass as a toast, then downed the last few swallows and put the glass on the counter. "I'm flatlined, and we have to be in the air by six." She pointed to the couch he'd napped on earlier. "That unfolds to a bed. Blankets are under it. Help yourself to anything in the kitchen or fresher."

He'd already been cooling his jets in her apartment for four hours. "I'll be fine." He stood and stretched. "Want that massage I owe you?"

"I'd love it, but I'd be asleep in three minutes." She smiled. "You do know the committee thinks you're my freelance recreational sex partner, don't you?"

"I figured." He gave her a saucy smile and wink. "I always wanted to be a boy toy."

She laughed. "I always wanted to be rich enough to afford one."

She locked the front and balcony doors, then wished him bright dreams and disappeared behind the sliding door of her bedroom.

He pulled out the blankets and decided it was too

much trouble to unfold the bed. He used the orajet gel he found in the fresher to clean his mouth and dirtied up one of her washcloths by wiping the ever-present dust off his face and neck. He'd make a lousy boy toy, but he wouldn't mind wrapping himself around warm, sensuous Anitra in her bed instead of sleeping on the lonely couch.

He made a face at himself in the mirror as he loosely knotted his braids on top of his head. Considering the way they'd parted, and given the current looming catastrophe, that seemed about as likely as winning the Nine Planets lottery.

The best thing he could do for now was get the *Diamantov* ready to fly again, and make it past the blockade with his own ship. Future miracles would have to wait.

## 3

**\* Interstellar Transit Point Blockade: CGC Military Frigate "Bassilon" \* GDAT 3233.047 \***

As the captain of the *Bassilon*, a well-armed peace frigate of Concordance Command's Space Division, Ivar Okeanos shouldn't have been filling in for the comms officer, who was the guest of honor at her own promotion-to-subcaptain celebration. Commodore Britton, head of the task group enforcing the quarantine blockade at the Polaris-Gamma system's interstellar transit jump point, would probably lecture him about maintaining the proper command distance. She liked lecturing, which was why Ivar assiduously avoided being in the same room with her. Daily realtime holo conferences were bad enough.

He also shouldn't have paid any attention to a large message packet queued in CPS Security Officer Paderau's data-space. While the Citizen Protection Service was a military division just like Space Div, Paderau wasn't in his chain of command, and could ignore any order from him unless it involved combat engagement or the immediate safety of the ship. However, as the CPS's representative, she could give him orders regarding his crew, including forcing them to submit to a telepathic interrogation if warranted. She could also, under the broadly-defined charter of keeping the galactic peace, order the ship to take questionable actions.

Unfortunately, Paderau was a dangerous combination of sly, obsessive, and ambitious, and heedless of standard military protocol. The only reason Okeanos noticed the message packet in the first place was because Paderau had left it open and unencrypted, and the shipcomp comms system had flagged six warning messages about it.

He absolutely shouldn't have read the packet. Getting caught would have cost him his recently awarded rank and first Space Div solo command. But the CPS security officers on all the task force's twenty ships had been burning up the bandwidth since the first day of the blockade, and Ivar's curiosity had gotten the better of him. He wished he hadn't read it, because now he had to do something about it.

Which was why he'd ordered a surprise inspection and hands-on test of *Bassilon*'s escape pods. The frigate had two hundred and twelve of them, and that didn't count the sealable engine and navigation pods that could act as escape pods, or the ten rapid-launch pinnace system ships in *Bassilon*'s mid-section.

The ship's subcaptains and commanders grumbled because each inspection took two people away from their regular shifts. *Bassilon* was currently seriously understaffed, which was why it had been sent to the easy-duty blockade to await incoming assignees. To show his command staff that he sympathized with their resource limitations, he volunteered himself and Subcaptain Nieth Sobek, his second-in-command, to pitch in.

The frigate's common spaces were always clean because of an army of cleaning bots, but the air in the corridor he and Sobek now traversed smelled stale. The hallway dead-ended at a dark and sealed emergency backup nav pod. According to *Bassilon*'s records, it had been overlooked in the last three rounds of escape-pod tests.

Ivar used the wallcomp to provide his biometric and key the sequence to activate the emergency pod. He hand-cranked the doors open, pleased that the analog mechanism was in smooth working order. He stood back and ushered Sobek in first, checking the wallcomp properly indicated her presence, then started it on a diagnostic program that would take nine minutes. He stepped inside and sealed the pod doors.

When he turned to look at Sobek, she was glaring at him, arms crossed. "Out with it, Ivar."

He didn't bother pretending he hadn't arranged the whole inspection program just so he could talk to her in one of the few unmonitored locations on the ship. She had nearly eighty years of experience in Space Div. After nine years serving with him, she knew him too well.

"Yesterday, I came across a packet of Paderau's that leads me to believe the CPS is using the settlement company's dispute with its settlers to institute a *de facto* regime change in the Polaris-Gamma government. Pol-G is a 'threat to the galactic peace' because it's been dragging its feet in applying for Concordance membership. It also refused to give the Concordance priority access to its unexpectedly abundant rare-earth metal deposits or the output of the flux fuel manufacturing facility they built under the ocean."

"Imagine that." Her tone was dry as a desert.

"Yeah, what a surprise. Unfortunately, any day now, we're going to be ordered to destroy, not just detain, a desperate, unarmed fleet of more than a *thousand* ships, not just two hundred, and that are carrying an estimated total of a hundred *thousand* refugees. Oh, and bonus, we get to let another fifty *thousand* people on the planet starve. Seems the settlement company lied about the remaining population by an order of magnitude, and the CPS knows it."

Sobek's expression and body language became unreadable. "What do you propose to do?"

He appreciated her propensity for cutting straight to the core. "I don't know yet." He walked around the center pillar to the nav console and powered it on. A small cloud of dust settled on his black-and-gray uniform sleeve. "Everything I've thought of so far tanks the career of everyone on this ship, or maybe even gets us killed." He brought up the old star charts to confirm their integrity, and while he was at it, grabbed the current charts from *Bassilon*'s primary nav comp. On strong impulse, he copied all the old charts back to the main shipcomp into an innocuous data hypercube. He'd learned to listen to his subconscious when it pushed like that.

Sobek unfolded the smaller console built into the

pillar, producing another cloud of dust. The pattern from
holo display cast her round face in blues and greens as she
manipulated the interface.

He called up the maintenance list from the networked
gauntlet he was never without and checked off the
completed items, as per Space Div procedures. He knew
Paderau read everything in his dataspace, sooner or later.
"If something happens to me, I hope you'll find a way to
get the word out." He drew his chin back to relieve the
gathering tension in his neck, to ward off another
headache. "You'd think the military would have learned
from the mass casualties it caused at Rashad Tarana, but
apparently not."

She gave him a sharp look. "You've chosen a very
hazardous star lane." She opened the environmental
controls. "Right now, Commodore Britton and Paderau
think you're an unimaginative traditionalist trying to live
down an unconventional military career and live up to a
semi-famous family name, but if you're caught, Paderau
will turn your mind inside out. She's not stupid."

"I'm well aware," he snapped. "Would you prefer we
demolish thousands of unarmored starships with
innocent colonists?" He took two measured breaths to
regain the lost reins of his temper. He was mad at the
situation, not at Sobek.

"Don't be dense. You've been keeping your head
down for so long that you've forgotten how to look up.
I'm telling you to use your intuition and your genius for
unorthodox strategy to figure out how to mitigate the
impending military disaster, and not fucking get caught."
She straightened up to rigid attention. "Sir."

"Hmph." He shook his head. He appreciated her rare bluntness. Usually she couched her advice as suggestions or alternatives, like philosophical puzzles. "You're the best second I've ever had. Don't go all stick-and-shine on me now."

She laughed. "I'm the *only* second you've had." She relaxed to her usual borderline slouch. "I don't envy your choices. Space Div can't take another public-relations nightmare. Everyone over the age of thirty still remembers the images of the Rashad Tarana survivors, and the realtime holovid of Subgeneral Ntombi's execution. Whether or not they know it, Space Division needs you."

Ivar shut down the nav systems. "I don't know about that, but those people deserve better than whatever the CPS has planned." He slammed closed the console with more force than was necessary. "Keep the galactic peace, my ass."

# 4

"No," said Gavril into his earwire, "the *other* X-one-eighty!" He blew out a frustrated breath as he watched the holo display of the work being done in the engine pod. How a certified system-drive design engineer managed not to know spatial directions was beyond him.

The newly enclosed nav pod of the *Diamantov* turned it into a proper emergency escape pod, but they still hadn't gotten the comms systems to connect, so Gavril and the refit team made do with earwires and a temporary secure net. Anitra had worked farkin' miracles in the last forty days to acquire the goods and services they needed, but competent, trustworthy ship specialists were hard to come by. It was a good thing liftoff was rumored to be two months away. Or three months, or six months, depending on who was talking.

The daily newstrends featured multiple stories of possible settlement company spies, with all minders being automatically suspect, or military spies out to sabotage the rumored but probably nonexistent planetary defenses. The Pol-G government blindly pretended business as usual, and did useless things like building more ground and air public transports, as if more settlers were coming, and mistakenly issuing four-hundred-liter, collapsible recycling crates to every adult and child on the planet, instead of one to each household.

Gavril didn't know about Pol-G's other cities, but he suspected Aetheres would explode when the government publicly announced the flight plan. Which was why he'd moved his trader ship to a hangar on the far side of the spaceport and added extra security measures. The polarized stay-versus-leave factions clashed often, sometimes violently. The burn-the-blight activists regularly torched vacant fields and empty buildings.

He wasn't looking forward to the trip into town that evening, but he'd promised Anitra he'd help her evaluate a cache of what she suspected were interstellar ship add-ons for luxury yachts, including a new-in-crate autodoc and a two-meter cargo container full of parts printers.

Thinking of Anitra reminded him he was supposed to have been practicing using his empath talent. He liked the lessons, mostly because they gave him a chance to spend quality time with her, but he was less fond of practicing by himself.

He cautiously extended his talent to try to determine who else was on the ship, and where they were. He'd made progress in the last two weeks—albeit uneven—by following Anitra's suggestions of things to try, such as finding a metaphor in his head for the sensations he experienced when using his talent. He didn't know if she didn't have time to give him more detailed lessons, or if that was her teaching method. She told him she couldn't compare his talent to her own or to previous trainees, since they'd had very different life paths. That was as close as she got to discussing anything of her history before Pol-G. He had the impression that whatever had sent her running to the frontier had been life-changing.

He already knew where Gulorom, the system drive engineer, was, so that was cheating. He extended his talent farther and discovered a glowing tangle of colored threads he recognized. It was half cheating, because he'd have been surprised if Navigator Lizet Asylkan wasn't around—she'd claimed one of the tiny crew quarters for her own and was staying on the ship with Gavril. She'd arrived the second day, a trader-family referral from Chief Ferrsi of Planetary Law Enforcement. Gavril liked Lizet, which was more than he could say for the other contractors they'd shuffled through the project. He reached out and tried to determine whether she was above him or below him, and how far. The ship's newly reinforced incalloy skeleton made his efforts more challenging.

Gulorom's voice in the earwire broke his concentration. *"Try it now."*

Gavril rotated the holo interface in front of him to focus on the system drives. "No change. Still only seeing three out of six coils." They'd added two coils to compensate for escaping Pol-G's gravity with full cargo holds.

Gulorom swore in her native Afro-French. *"I'll ping you when I'm ready for another test."*

Gavril's stiff back complained loudly enough to make him get up and walk small circles around the navigator seat, twisting from side to side as he did. His regular exercise routine had gone by the wayside since he'd gotten stuck on Pol-G, and he was paying for it now. He promised himself that once he got his own ship back, with its well-equipped exercise room, everything would go back to normal. He wished he knew when that would be. Or that he was sure he wanted it anymore.

Lizet pinged his earwire. *"I'm hitting the MODs hold. Want anything?"* Though the galley now worked perfectly, they were too busy to use it, and mostly subsisted on a cargo hold full of ready-made mealpacks, or meals of the day, as Lizet called them. The double-wide container full of mealpacks had come from his ship. The cost of the cargo was a small price to pay for the return of his livelihood.

"No, Anitra is taking me out for dinner tonight." They'd maintained the fiction of a non-professional relationship to give them cover for their clandestine scouting activities.

"Lucky you. Ask her if she's heard anything about Uncle Setro."

"Will do." Lizet's uncle was a pilot with a big merchant ship, and both had vanished two weeks ago. The family was understandably worried.

In the pilot's quarters, Gavril dressed in his lucky blue jacket and the nicer clothes he'd retrieved from his own ship, but packed work clothes and toiletries in an overnight bag, as though he expected to spend the night with his casual hot-connect sex partner. If it had been real, he admitted to himself, it wouldn't be casual, at least on his part. But the timing tanked.

He selected one of the dozens of vehicles that Anitra had redirected to the ship dock for warehousing. The planetary weather AI predicted rain, so he went with the lumbering but rock-steady ground hauler, in case the cache needed emptying that evening. Best to be prepared in case the universe was in a generous mood.

SEVENTY MINUTES LATER, he met Anitra in the lobby of a well-lit, inviting restaurant on the ground floor of a multi-use building. He greeted her with a warm kiss, partly for their cover, and partly because he wanted to. She was a fascinating, strong, and sexy woman who fired his jets.

At their table, he poured water for them both from the filtered pitcher. "I like your tunic. It suits you." The layers of turquoise blue and floral gold hugged her figure and accentuated her rounded breasts and narrow waist. Flashes of gold and copper in her dark hair and makeup gave her an artistic flare. He could easily imagine her being the star of an exclusive art show.

"Thanks. I was tired of the corporate suits." She nodded toward him. "You look great in that vest." She gave him a rakish smile. "Very pirate clan."

He laughed to cover his surprise. The embroidered and pieced vest of hand-woven fabrics was one of the few things he had of his long-dead father's, who had indeed been pirate clan. He didn't mention it often because it made customs inspectors nervous and Space Div surly. He didn't remember mentioning it to Anitra during their previous fling, either, but he didn't remember everything the way filers did. If he had to be a minder, he would have preferred that talent, or Anitra's shields, over his unruly empath talent.

None of the twenty or thirty other restaurant patrons were broadcasting at the moment, but all it would take is one public argument to make everyone tense, and Gavril's shaky containment would be overwhelmed. Anitra had told him that most empaths thrived on people and physical contact, and maybe that was true, but he didn't like them in groups.

Mindful of the public venue, he and Anitra chatted about trivia. Fortunately, the food was good, and plentiful enough for him to take a carton back to the ship for Lizet.

Anitra paid the tab without wincing at the superorbital prices, making him wonder if the government reimbursed her expenses, or she had funds of her own. He resolutely told himself it wasn't his business. She hadn't asked anything about his finances.

He'd had to park the ground hauler three blocks away, but it was close enough to walk. The neighborhood was a combination of commercial and light industrial. Unrepaired scars from street vehicles marred the glass pavement, and of course, the ubiquitous white dust was everywhere, like spattered powdered sugar. The roads were unexpectedly devoid of ground traffic.

They turned a corner westward, which put them walking into the wind. The afternoon's brief rain left lingering humidity, making it feel colder than fall should be. He sealed his jacket, and Anitra tightened her scarf.

An echo, or a smell, or maybe a brush against his talent caught his attention. He certainly felt it when Anitra dropped her shield. Multiple threads of anger teased the edges of his talent.

"Riot," they both said almost together as they slowed.

"Coming this way," she added.

He glanced up the street toward where the threads originated, but didn't see anything. "Let's go back to the restaurant."

They turned around and headed back the way they'd come, walking quickly.

She stumbled, but righted herself. "These shoes are cursed." She slowed a little. "Last time I wore them, we had a freak storm, and I had to tromp through forty centimeters of snow."

"I can carry you." He unexpectedly flashed on a memory of carrying her, laughing, into the bedroom of the hotel where they'd lived for a week. He'd loved the strength of her under her womanly curves.

She chuckled. "No need, but thanks for the offer."

More threads of anger pushed at his talent, and he got a whiff of something burning. He glanced up to the west, but the height of the buildings blocked any view.

They heard the first distant shouts just as they half-ran across the street to the restaurant.

The moment they got inside, she sent him to find the

manager while she convinced the greeter to lock the front door.

He only saw servers out front, so he walked straight back into the kitchen area.

A roly-poly man in green moved to intercept Gavril and made vigorous shooing motions toward him. "You go back and sit down." His English was heavily accented with Mandarin. "Servers take care of you."

Gavril shook his head. "There's a riot coming this way. You need to close up."

The man's eyes widened in shock, and Gavril felt the man's rising panic. "No riots here!" He looked to the chef in pale pink. "They said no riots!"

"Well, there's one now." Gavril put steel in his voice. "Go turn out the front lights."

The manager hesitated, then pushed past Gavril and headed into the dining area. Gavril turned to the chef in pink. "If you have a back door, lock it, and turn out any street lights. From what I've seen, looters take advantage of riots."

The chef quickly ordered one of his staff to comply. They were a calmer lot, perhaps because their high-stress kitchen environment better prepared them for emergencies.

Gavril hesitated, then went out front to find Anitra. The tension in the room pushed on his talent's containment as he threaded his way to the front. The manager and the greeter argued with hissed whispers, pointing to the window wall that faced the street. The customers at nearby tables watched them warily.

He found Anitra looking out the front door. She

turned to him and stepped close. "Are you up for trying an intermediate lesson?" She touched her temple, to mean his empath talent. "We need to project calm, especially to the manager."

He shifted his weight uneasily. "I don't know how."

"Yes, you do, but you don't know you're doing it." She slipped her hand into his. "Feel this." She dropped her shields, and a subtle blue of calm brushed by him. "Now this." Shades of orange and pink comfort mixed into the blue strands. She leaned into him in half embrace, her mouth next to his ear. "Those aren't my feelings, they're reflections of yours. Well, some of them. You're also worried and annoyed, and skeptical."

He put his arm around her waist and spoke quietly. "It feels out of focus."

She nodded. "Probably because you're stronger than I am." She darted a glance toward the manager, who was now stabbing at a wallcomp, darkening random lights in the restaurant. She touched the center of his chest. "Find those confident and happy parts of you and share them with him. Sometimes, it helps to think of something relaxing you want him to enjoy, too. Not sex—that's too hard to control."

"I'll try," he said, hoping he didn't screw it up. He was vain enough to want to impress her.

He concentrated on the tangled skein of grays of worry and whites of fear that came from the manager, mixed with a few threads of blue for confidence and ochre for pride. Gavril thought of a deep-tissue massage, of how soothing it felt to ease tight muscles, then tried to weave the purplish hue of contentment into the manager's skein. Surprisingly, it worked. Inspired, he used his talent to tug on the blue and ochre threads, to bring them to the top.

"Not so fast," whispered Anitra. "Don't want him to feel chemmed."

He concentrated on nudging the grays and whites aside to make room for the brighter colors.

"Good. Now see if you can do the same for the greeter."

The greeter was less agitated, so it was easier to push away the grays of worry and the green of exasperation in favor of the underlying confident blue.

"Yes, you've got it." Anitra smiled. "You're better than you think."

He smiled and tightened his arm on her waist. "Are you helping?"

"No... Oh, frelling hell."

He followed her gaze out the glass door. Flames rose from behind the rooftops across the street. The restaurant's soundproofing blocked any street noise.

She pointed to the front window. "The restaurant is still lit up like a Solstice Day display."

Gavril let go of Anitra to cross to the manager. "Kill the lights and the sign now, or we'll be a shiny egg to crack."

The manager shook his head. "The sign is run by the building's computer." He pointed to the ceiling. "No controls here."

Anitra stepped up. "Can you black the window wall? Or at least dim the lights up front?"

The nearby greeter shook her head. "The wall only

goes to gray." She frowned at the thick glass. "They'll see any inside lights." She tilted her head toward the dining area. "It's not safe to leave people in the dark."

"Do what you can," said Gavril.

As the greeter and the manager turned back to the wallcomp, Anitra slipped her hand in Gavril's and pulled him toward the door.

"Advanced lesson. See if you can tell where the rioters are, how many are in the group, and if they're coming this way."

He didn't want his talent anywhere near an angry crowd, but he'd like being attacked by well-armed looters even less. He closed his eyes and reached out with his talent.

Anitra squeezed his hand. "Eyes open. Don't make yourself unnecessarily vulnerable."

He opened his eyes to look out the darkening door glass. His talent found the roiling tangles of clashing colors. He made himself glide over the grasping, glowing skeins to get a sense of numbers.

"Feels like the crowd in the tax office, so a hundred fifty, maybe two hundred?" He glanced at her. "There's a big knot of them northeast of here, but a smaller band of them moving south and west." He pointed out the window toward the roadway intersection. "Coming from there, I think."

"The fire will drive some of them away, but not enough." She frowned. Though he wasn't focused on her, his wide-open talent told him she was deeply worried and wary. "I can protect us, but I'll need your help, and I can't answer questions. You'll have to trust me."

He sensed fear in her, but he trusted she knew her capabilities. "Okay."

A small thread of relief surfaced in the fascinating skein of her emotions. "If you can keep the people in here from panicking, I'll do what I can to keep the rioters uninterested in the restaurant."

"How will... sorry." He grimaced. "Any suggestions on how to keep thirty people calm, when I'm not?"

"Drift around them, or whatever metaphor works for you, but don't get caught up in them—that's the siren song for all empaths. Send them calm, like what you did with the manager. Keep an eye out for spikes of whatever colors you see that mean fear, because that cascades downhill fast. If you find any minders who notice what you're doing, skip over them if you can, or send them apologetic feelings. If you find other empaths, they might be willing to help." She glanced grimly toward the door. "Keep everyone away from me, if you can."

He started to step away, but she stopped him. "Not you." She touched the side of his face. "You're my anchor."

The complex colors of her emotional skein flared. Before he had time to interpret them, they desaturated as she turned to face the door.

He turned to face the dining area and crossed his arms, mimicking a vigilant enforcer, though he wasn't dressed for the part. He reached out with his talent to get a feel for what he was up against. The clumps of threads called out to his talent, but he managed to ignore the individuals in favor of the group. He thought of it as multi-hued fog. Wariness predominated, with clouds of anger and fear, and smaller clouds of determination and contentment, mostly from what he took to be the kitchen staff. The characteristic oasis of darkness told him one of the diners was a shielder.

He tried borrowing the calmer colors from the kitchen staff and pushing them into the larger fog, but it had no effect. The white of fear flared closer to him. The manager stood near the darkened window wall, looking out. His wide eyes and frozen expression reflected in the glass.

Gavril couldn't spare the focus to keep the manager calm. He edged closer to the greeter and caught her attention. "Tell the manager the kitchen needs him."

She nodded and approached the manager as Gavril went back to his self-appointed position at Anitra's back.

He extended his talent again and felt the fear-white wave of the manager as he navigated around the tables of diners.

Determination surfaced in Anitra's threads, making him want to find out what she was doing. He resolutely turned his talent to the diners and their billows of color. Since his contentment technique worked with the manager, he called up the sense memory of a massage and visualized sending it like a gentle breeze into the fog. After several long moments, he was gratified to see a subtle shift, darkening from fear white to wary dull brown.

He wafted through the fog, sharing his contentment turquoise wherever he found the duller colors. He hunched his shoulders against the increasingly painful tingling of clashing colors behind him, which had to be the rioters. They ebbed and flowed, but none of them bunched or slowed nearby. Soothing them was well beyond his barely beginner abilities.

He forced himself to ignore everything but the diners in the restaurant and the cooks in the kitchen, shaping himself to fit into their much more pleasant fog. To his talent, the shielder he'd noticed before kept moving around, and it took him a bit to reconcile what his eyes told him. The shielder was one of the servers.

Gavril lost track of time, tending the foggy mists before him and ignoring the pins and needles behind him. He was soaked with sweat by the time Anitra touched his arm. "You can pull back now."

The pins and needles were gone. He spent agonizing moments trying to reel his talent back in, but his weak containment failed. That disability had driven him to become a trader who spent days and weeks in transit with no other humans around to stress him. He closed his eyes, but it only made things worse. Anger rose in him, and suddenly, he was seeing it start to affect the colors in the fog. "Fark!"

He felt her touch on his arm again. "Do you need a shield?"

He clenched his jaw hard and nodded.

Her shield descended over him like a dark net. His over-stimulated talent fought to be free, but he tensed every muscle he had until the talent retreated, like a sullen child, into the corner of his mind.

He opened his eyes and found her standing in front of him, shielding him with her body as well as her mind. She looked pale, with bruised eyes, like she hadn't slept in a week.

"Are you sick?" He pushed his damp hair off his forehead.

"Blowback." She glanced up at the planetary time display on the wall, then back to him. "It'll pass."

He gave her a puzzled look that invited her to explain.

"Talent overuse often causes negative physical feedback." She tilted her chin toward his chest, where his shirt was soaked. "You drip like a rainforest. I get sinus congestion."

He turned and moved closer to the restaurant's darkened window wall. He felt Anitra step up next to him as he looked out. The buildings across the street looked scarred, like someone had thrown acid. The roadway was unaccountably wet in spots.

Anitra pointed toward the still visible flames to the west. "The fire crew turned the water on the rioters. They dispersed." She rubbed her eyes. Her voice sounded nasal and muffled. "The police issued a lockdown for all transportation and businesses in the area."

He rolled his tense shoulders and neck, trying to relax. "I need to get away from people." Exhaustion washed through him, and the night was far from over.

## 5

* Polaris-Gamma * GDAT 3233.054 *

Anitra stood in the pooled light from a building spotlight, near the gaping, beamer-blackened entrance to the storage unit, waiting for Gavril to bring the ground hauler around. He'd offered, and she'd accepted. Her feet hurt from her cursed shoes almost as much as her head.

She was out of practice exercising the full extent of her minder talents, and now she was paying the price. Her sinuses felt like someone injected them with solidified road glass. She probably deserved it for pushing Gavril into using his uncontrolled talent before he was ready. He'd retreated to the thorny side of his personality that made others give him a wide berth. She'd have preferred to avoid him, too, or at least activate her shields and ignore him, but she worried she wouldn't be able to tell if he was in trouble, because he certainly wouldn't tell her.

He'd obviously never experienced blowback before, and didn't know what to look out for.

The ugly ground hauler had survived the rioters, probably because it already looked broken down, but that had been the end of her good luck for the evening. In between her initial surveillance of the storage unit and tonight's midnight visit, someone else had found it and cleaned it out. As it was the third such theft in a row, she'd have to be a farking flatliner not to assume someone was using her as an unwitting hunting dog to snap up desirable goods.

The only people she figured she could exonerate were Gavril and the young navigator, Lizet Asylkan, because they could have easily waited for the cargo to come to them when she finally sent it. Planetary Police Chief Ferrsi had the resources to monitor her activities, but he had the whole planet to choose from for lucrative targets, not just the small finds she'd tracked down in and near Aetheres and squirreled away all over the city. At least the thieves hadn't yet found her caches.

Unfortunately, her thief suspect list included her supply depot staff, city transportation department employees, any of the freighter ship refit contractors, anyone on the escape committee, or a minder with a finder talent who had sensed her pattern and told theft crews where to raid. On top of everything else that kept her up at night, now she had to figure out how to hide her activities and still do her job. She wasn't cut out to be a spy, and hated clandestine bullshit. She'd had enough of that at the end of her former career with the Citizen Protection Service to last a lifetime.

The lumbering, rattling hauler pulled up, and she climbed in. She sat up front next to Gavril in the humid, darkened cab and webbed herself into the co-driver seat. The smell of mold was strong enough to make it past her stopped-up sinuses.

He brought up a holo map from the city's traffic control system. "Know any good chems and alterants shops between here and your building? I'll need oreznil to sleep tonight."

"No, sorry." She knew he wouldn't like her next words. "It's not a good idea to get warped when you're recovering from blowback. It messes with your containment."

"I don't *have* any fucking containment." His irritation buffeted her empathic senses.

Chaos, but she was tempted to use her talent to smooth out the bitter flavor of his resentment, but it would destroy what little trust he had in her. "Chems can flatten your talent, but they make you vulnerable to any telepath who wants to poke around. When the CPS interrogates high-level empaths, they use Pazi Nidrasom, the nova-strength version of oreznil, so they can't focus long enough to defend themselves."

He entered her building's coordinates into the ground hauler's navigation system with stabbing fingers and sent the request to the traffic control system. Ten seconds later, the TCS took control of the hauler and moved them out into the sparse traffic.

His sharp anger finally abated, leaving simmering irritation. She closed her eyes and leaned her head against the side window. She needed about twelve hours of sleep, and was likely to get less than six.

"How can an empath defend against a telepath?" The scorn in his tone reminded her how little he appreciated his talent. She supposed she'd feel the same, if it had driven her away from people she liked, and brought nothing but overwhelming pain.

"Flood the telepath with distracting emotions. You're strong enough to manufacture it in them by will alone." She lifted one shoulder. "I have to use my own emotions or reflections from emotional people nearby."

He made a rude sound. "I tried that in the restaurant. It didn't work."

She tried for a reasonable tone. "You can learn."

An acid wash of anger was her only warning when he suddenly brought his full empath talent to bear on her. He wanted her as mad as he was, mad enough to give him a fight. Survival hormones flooded her brain, narrowing her focus and sending her heart racing. She struggled to raise her shields against his formidable strength, and finally sealed him out.

She took deep, slow breaths to reinforce her shields and regain some semblance of her equanimity. He wasn't the first student to have ever lashed out at her, but coming from him, it hurt. A lot. She counted to one hundred, and then again, visualizing each number in her mind's eye, to give her body a chance to ramp back down.

She finally turned her seat to look at him. Her shields prevented her from sensing his feelings, and she couldn't see his expression in the dark hauler cab as he watched the hauler's navigation console. At that moment, she didn't really care.

"That was your one and only free pass." She spoke quietly and precisely. "You're hurting, you're still experiencing blowback, and you don't know your own strength." She waited until he turned to look at her. "If you ever do anything like that to me again, I'll put you in lockdown on your ship until launch day, even if that's six months from now. Do you understand?"

He turned to her, anguish on his face. "I'm sorry–"

She cut him off. "Do. You. Understand?" She ground out each word.

His posture straightened, and his remorseful expression faded to unreadable. "Yes. I understand."

She held his gaze a moment longer, then turned away. The console's countdown said only ten minutes left until they got to her building. A hot shower before bed would help clear her sinus congestion, but wouldn't mend her heart.

Her government percomp startled her with the vibration and tone of an incoming private ping. She listened to the message in her earwire.

*"This is an unannounced drill for the emergency response team. You are instructed to report to your designated command center by zero two hundred hours, and bring your player handbook."*

The message from Chief Enforcer Ferrsi repeated itself, then ended. The escape committee's cover was disaster preparedness, but they'd never met at two in the frickin' morning.

"Trouble?" asked Gavril. He must have noticed her listening to the message.

"I don't know." She pointed to the navigation console. "I need the nearest public transport kiosk that calls autocabs." She used her government percomp to order the autocab, and entered the special code that encrypted her pickup and designation coordinates.

He immediately rerouted the hauler. Three minutes later, the hauler's console signaled arrival and slowed to a halt.

She sealed her coat and pulled up her hood. "I'll ping you with news when I can."

"You'll be warmer if you wait in here."

His peace offering tempted her, but she was too wrung out to take it. "It's only a couple of minutes. I'll be all right. You've got an hour's drive back to the ship." She opened the hauler's side door and clambered out, nearly turning her ankle because of her damned, bad-luck shoes.

She watched the ground hauler pull away. Turning away, she wrapped her arms around herself against the cold, and against the overwhelming sense of loss. Her trust had been abused, and she'd lost Gavril's affection, which she wasn't sure she'd ever had in the first place.

HAZY DAWN HAD CREPT over Aetheres by the time she stumbled into her apartment. Her life had gone from merely stressful to full-blown chaotic in the space of three hours.

She pinged Gavril and Lizet at the repair dock and asked them to come to her apartment immediately, but to stay off the traffic control system. She threw her cursed shoes in the recycler, wishing she could watch them burn, then showered and put on painting clothes and running boots. If she was going to have to face the end of the world with no sleep, at least she'd be comfortable, for once.

She brewed the last of her real coffee and foraged in her kitchen to pull together a haphazard breakfast for herself and her guests. She'd just pulled out plates and utensils when Lizet pinged their arrival on the rooftop airpad. To have gotten there so fast, they'd probably flown the repossessed racing flitter. She ushered them in a few minutes later and pointed to the breakfast bar.

"Eat, or it'll go to waste."

She dug into a plate full of fluffy scrambled eggs and reheated breaded fish, eating as fast as she could to stave off the waves of exhaustion that threatened to take her down.

Gavril, handsome as ever, looked calm and collected, despite the fact that he was clearly wearing sleep pants and an engineer's tunic under his pullover sweater. Black-haired, ash-pale Lizet wore charcoal gray everything, and looked both nervous and excited. Gavril said she was an extraordinarily talented navigator, for being only sixteen.

Anitra took a deep breath. "Liftoff is the day after tomorrow." She took several gulps of her cooled coffee. "As of an hour ago, the planetary traffic control system, and the weather and local comms satellites are simultaneously 'down for maintenance'"—she made air quotes with her fingers—"and blocking outgoing comms to the system's CGC comms satellite. The ground-based disaster communications networks are fully functional and activated, but each of the three settled continents has its own."

"Why now?" asked Gavril.

"Because Chief Ferrsi's best intel says someone high up is a settlement company spy who's getting too close to discovering there really *is* an evacuation plan, not just a dysfunctional, flailing government rearranging the deck chairs. The committee is damn lucky the 'red herrings and rumors' campaign worked for as long as it did."

"How are they going to get everyone off the planet?" Lizet looked to the ceiling, as if she could see ships overhead.

Gavril shook his head. "They won't have to. I'll bet at least fifteen percent refuse to leave."

"More like twenty-five percent. Settlers are stubborn." Anitra poured herself another cup of coffee, and took a piece of buttered toast to keep her stomach from complaining. "The coordinators are using the disaster comms network to tell people what they can take and where to go. The traffic system will route people to their assigned ships." She turned to Lizet. "Which reminds me. Your missing uncle is with his ship on the west coast of South Nacrilo, near Serenum. They've been moving ships away from our spaceport as much as possible, in case the settlement company or the military does something sneaky." She quirked a smile. "They even printed shells to look like the ships, to fool orbital surveillance."

Gavril frowned. "Assuming we all make it past the blockade, which is a damn big 'if,' where are we going? Or is it every ship for itself?"

"Biggest secret there is." She made herself eat a bite of her toast. "The committee members hate not knowing. Dalgono, my boss, and his allies on the committee aren't happy about only two days' notice, either." She held up her left wrist to show them her new government-issued bracelet percomp that looked a lot like a parole tracker. "They *really* hate that all of us committee members are being safety-monitored until liftoff. That's why I asked you to come to me. I didn't want to risk giving away the location of the repair dock."

Lizet tore a strip off her paper napkin. "What about the *Diamantov*?"

Anitra sighed. "We'd need another month to make it spaceworthy, and I never found a pilot, much less a crew. Saving people comes first."

Gavril and Lizet exchanged a look. Lizet tore another strip off her napkin. Gavril cleared his throat. "About that..."

Anitra raised an eyebrow.

Lizet focused on her napkin shredding as she spoke. "Remember that twisty guy, early on, who said he was a metal fabricator, but turned out he didn't know incalloy from iron? He asked a lot of questions before Gav fired him." She glanced up through her bangs at Anitra, then down again.

Anitra shook her head in confusion. "I'm not following."

Gavril crossed his arms. "We've been lying to everyone, including you, about how far along we are. We told the other contractors the ship repair is a scam, and that we think you're secretly using it to siphon funds from a wealthy zero-head who thinks it's their family's ticket off the planet. We said we didn't care, because a job's a job."

"Why would you... Oh." She waved apologetically. "Spies. Theft crews. Scammers. Sorry, I'm slow this morning." She put her elbow on the counter and rested her chin on her fist. "So, tell me about the *Deset Diamantov*."

Gavril got up from his stool at the breakfast bar to retrieve his tablet. "This is what everyone thinks." He displayed a very familiar holo diagram of the ship showing progress on the various repairs, with long lists in mostly red and gray to indicate incomplete status. He manipulated the interface, and the list of repairs faded, leaving a few items, with only two in caution status. "This is reality. We can work around the comms problem. Top off the flux and system drive fuel, and the *Diamantov* could lift off today."

"This is stunning." She stared in awe at the slowly rotating holo of the ancient freighter. "You've done more with the ship than I'd have ever thought possible." Tears threatened as she gave them a watery smile. "I'm sorry we can't see it fly."

"Lizet and I had a long talk this morning." Gavril tilted his head toward the young woman. "After your midnight meeting, we figured something was up." Gavril enveloped Anitra's cold fingers in his warm hand. "Get us the cargo and four crew with interstellar transit experience. I'll be loadmaster and prime pilot, Lizet will be navigator and second pilot, and we'll hope the blockade folds in the face of an unorganized, unarmed, thousand-ship fleet of refugees."

Gavril's expression showed stubborn determination. Lizet looked up with hope in her eyes.

Anitra straightened up and met Gavin's gaze. "Who'll pilot *your* ship?"

Gavril looked to Lizet.

"My cousin Tamazo," she said. "He doesn't have a cert because he's only fifteen, but he's got more hours than most commercial pilots twice his age. My family vouched for him, and Gav... uh, Mr. Danilovich agreed."

Gavril nodded when Anitra sent him a questioning look. "Better another trader with good recommendations than some random amateur pilot who needs an AI assist just to find the fresher."

Anitra turned to Lizet. "And what does your family think about you going on the *Diamantov*, instead of with them?" In her experience, trader families were clannish and very protective of their offspring.

"They said I'm old enough to plot my own star chart. I want to go with you." She began braiding her napkin shreds. "I'm a minder. Just a filer, but my father..." She swallowed whatever she'd been going to say. "Mr. Danilovich says you and he are minders, too."

Anitra wanted to hug the too-skinny, diffident young woman and tell her it'd get better, but realistically, it probably wouldn't. Most days, prejudice against minders felt like a part of civilization's DNA.

Gavril squeezed Anitra's fingers, then let go. "Her grandmother said it'd be better not to put all the family treasures in one ship." He glanced at Lizet. "They trust her. So do I."

Anitra closed her eyes for a moment, then looked straight at Gavril. "You don't like people, and you're not enamored of me right now, either. Why are you doing this?"

"Because I owe you." Gavril held her gaze. "Not just because I was a colossal, selfish jackhole last night, but because refitting the *Diamantov* gave me something good to do. I was on the path to chemming myself into a medical center or mind shop because I couldn't stand the crowds." He paused, then continued. "You knew that, and trusted me anyway."

"You trusted me, too, even though it was a fantastical idea," she said softly. "Both of you. I appreciate that more than you'll ever know." She wiped away a tear that fell.

Lizet peeked up through the black hair that usually obscured her pale blue eyes. "You're not torqued about us telling everyone you're running a twist?"

"Not at all." Anitra smiled tiredly. "I'm not devious. If you'd told them the truth, someone would have stolen the ship in the first ten-day." She shook her head. "I'm too idealistic for my own good."

Gavril topped off her coffee. "The galaxy needs people with dreams. You inspire the rest of us." His sweet, serious smile made her heart skip a beat.

"So are you going to do it?" asked Lizet. "Can I stay?"

"Yes." Anitra took a deep breath and let it out slowly, then looked at Lizet. "And yes." She pulled her tablet out of her pocket and unfolded it. "First, can the *Diamantov* take more people than just the four crew you asked for? It'll be easier to get my hidden stockpiles to the ship if I can offer an evacuation berth for the people who transport them to you."

Gavril squinted at the holo of the ship. "Yeah, maybe eighteen if they don't mind shift sleeping on pads and eating mealpacks. And if they don't bring every stinking thing they own."

"They'll travel light." Anitra added a note about the crew limit on one of her myriad lists. "Remember those household recycling crates the government issued, that everyone thought was a bureaucratic screw-up because everyone got one? The evacuation orders will restrict each person to whatever can fit in one crate."

Lizet's jaw dropped. "We got those right after the court judgment came down. They were planning this for a whole year?"

Anitra nodded. "*Two* years. The committee was started by forecasters who predicted a lot of this. Not the details, like the blight or the mysteriously malfing CGC comms satellites when the court case was registered. But they were right that the settlement company would cheat and escalate, and the Pol-G government would tell them to suck flux, and the military would come, and the planet would probably be lost." She rolled her eyes. "Not that they came out and said all that, though, because it would have influenced the chess pieces—that's us mere mortals —and warped their precious forecasts."

Gavril's finger tapped a beat on his chin. "We've got the right substrate for the parts printers. We could string habitat systems to any of the small holds to make group living quarters, but we wouldn't have enough escape pods if things go wrong." He made the display zoom in on the ship's center. "We'd need a good environment engineer and a couple of extra experienced crew to run everything. The shipcomp's AI is too new to handle retro kludges."

Lizet raised her hand. "Uhm, sirs? Captains?"

Anitra blinked, then laughed. "She's definitely talking to you, Trader Captain Danilovich. I'm just, er, Supply Master and Logistics."

Gavril smiled briefly. "Yes, Navigator and Pilot-in-Training Asylkan?"

"My maternal great grandparents are staying behind because they think the government won't allow pets, even if they're valuable." She pushed her asymmetrical bangs behind one ear, revealing her elfin face. "Before the family settled on Pol-G, Great-Grandfather Maruk was a master environment engineer, and Great-Grandfather Sinjin designed flux engines. I think they'd come with us if you let them bring their cats and dogs."

Anitra didn't need her empath talent to see Lizet's worry and sadness. "How many cats and dogs?"

Lizet dropped her gaze. "Eighteen, I think. Maybe twenty-six, if Chaos Seven had her kittens."

Anitra looked to Gavril, who put up his hands and shook his head. "Logistics is your star lane."

Anitra made a snap decision. "Ask them. Be honest about the risks, especially the escape pod problem. If they still want to come, they can bring their pets." She pointed toward the percomp on Lizet's arm. "If you trust them to keep a secret, ping them now. Otherwise, wait for the evac order."

Lizet's broad smile, the first Anitra had seen from her, lit up her face with the promise of future beauty. "They live in the country. They don't have anyone to tell." She stepped away from the breakfast bar to send the message.

Anitra shuddered as a sudden wave of exhaustion coursed through her. She closed her eyes for a moment. When she opened them again, Gavril was standing only centimeters in front of her, his face full of concern.

"I'll trade you," he said. "You sleep for three hours. Lizet and I will call people we trust to be crew or cargo drivers. We'll run errands for you in town. I'll hit a chems shop for safe ramper drugs, because we'll probably need them."

"It's a lovely idea, but I'd sleep through any alarms, and I can't afford the lost time." Acid curdled her stomach. "I'll eat more protein and sleep later."

Gavril cradled her face with his warm hands. "You're no good to us if you're impaired." He brushed a thumb along her cheekbone. "I have your door codes. I promise I'll come back here and wake you myself by zero nine hundred."

He was right about exhaustion impairing her judgment. She cupped one of his hands with hers. "Okay." She dropped her mental shields and sent him an empathic message of gratitude blended with respect. He sent her worry and determination, spiced with protective satisfaction.

"Sleep." He kissed her forehead, then let her go. "I'll put the food away."

She'd made no close friends since landing on Pol-G, so she'd forgotten the bone-deep comfort of having someone looking out for her.

She stumbled off to bed to do as she was told. Life would be coming at her with all blasters blazing soon enough.

# 6

The countdown in the *Diamantov*'s navigation pod chimed four bell-like tones because Gavril liked the sound better than a nagging synthvoice telling him the time.

Lizet's voice came over the earwire. *"Supply Master Helden's ping says she's inbound with cargo on a tread-mounted public transport."* Lizet was their acting comms officer until liftoff, when her navigator job would begin. *"She sent sizes and estimated masses to your dataspace."*

"She's driving it?" Anitra's many laudable talents did not include operating ground-based vehicles, especially those the size of a small city block. He feared for the few still-standing buildings along her route. From what he'd heard from the newstrends, yesterday's riots had been vicious. He was very glad to be many kilometers away from Aetheres.

*"I think she got the traffic control system to do it. She said her ETA is fifty-three minutes."*

"Okay, notify the crew. And tell your elders to get the nursery habitat off Anitra's bunk."

Lizet said she would and disconnected.

He and Anitra would be sharing the captain's quarters, such as they were. Since she'd waited until the last possible minute to leave for the ship, her fold-down padded bed had been given over in the interim to Chaos Seven and her new kittens. Gavril stayed in the incalloy-clad nav pod because it helped contain his troublesome, good-for-nothing talent that had nearly gotten him iced by Anitra.

In the two days since the morning meeting in her apartment, he had worked hard to redeem himself by making the *Diamantov* as ready and resilient as he could. He'd also given some thought to how they could get maximum cash and trade value for the eclectic cargo she'd amassed.

She'd made clever use of the repair dock's incorrect "transportation warehouse" label to help clear abandoned vehicles out of the public transport routes. In the chaos of the evacuation, no one noticed the abandoned vehicles made an extra stop or two at Anitra's hidey-holes, or that they were operated by a few of Gavril's acquaintances and more of the Asylkan family's friends, all of whom just happened to have commercial ship crew experience and wanted a guaranteed liftoff berth enough to take a chance on the freighter.

*Diamantov*'s crew was as eclectic as her cargo, and

acted more like freelance pirate clan than regulation anything, but Gavril thought they'd be able to launch at the end of the coordinated liftoff window. Lizet's great-grandfathers had done amazing work with the environmental systems. They'd even built and populated a nascent aquaponics system to supplement the more conventional atmosphere exchangers, and were teaching the shipcomp's AI what to monitor.

Only the chaos-bedeviled comms system stubbornly refused all efforts to make it behave. As a last resort, Gavril had fitted the repair dock's army of cleaning and maintenance bots with spools of comms fiber and ran them throughout the ship. The result was a primitive, local comms net that only worked with shipcomp earwires. It was one step up from cups and string, but better than nothing.

He brought up the manifest of the final plunder... er, supplies coming in with Anitra. After he cataloged them, he tapped his ship earwire to ping Cargo Handler Elongo, who was also the crew's medic by virtue of her first-responder-team training. "Incoming cargo has a used autodoc and related crates of chems. Find Engineer Vasak and figure out where we can hook it up. The closer to crew quarters, the better."

His percomp pinged him with a reminder to eat. He determinedly ignored the pressure of a thousand more important things as he pulled out one of the mealpacks he'd stowed in the nav pod. Good chems and short naps helped him stay alert, but they only worked if he ate like a biometal-enhanced, elite-forces Jumper on shore leave.

He triggered the heater and shoveled the protein substitute and reconstituted vegetable lumps into his mouth as fast as he could chew and swallow. He promised himself a real meal once the ship went transit.

All across the planet, ships had been launching for the last four hours, including his trader ship, which was piloted by Lizet's prodigy cousin and stuffed to the rafters with thirty-eight people. And because it was his personal ship, he allowed the passengers to take their pets, defying the specific prohibition in the government's evacuation order. According to the last ping, they'd cleared the atmosphere fifteen minutes ago.

They and the hundreds of other ships skulked in the shadow of Pol-G or one of its three misshapen moons, waiting to make the mass move toward the system's interstellar transit jump point. All they'd need were the intended destination codes—still the biggest secret on or off the planet—and the military blockade to fold in the face of so many unarmed ships full of innocent civilians fleeing an ecological disaster.

AN HOUR later found him on the loadmaster platform of the subterranean dock, supervising the bots and crew at the *Diamantov*'s biggest loading bay below. It was faster to use humans to offload Anitra's battered bus for anything they could carry to the automated grav carts, and leave the heavy lifting to the mismatched load bots. Anitra had apparently been saving the best for last, because in addition to the autodoc, her cargo had a huge variety of printing substrates, enough cases of high-quality mealpacks to take them to the Andromeda Galaxy and back, and densely packed containers of refined rare-earth minerals that would net a small fortune in the right auction.

Anitra waved at him as she headed into the monster airlock—so named because someone had painted the interior side to look like the gaping maw of a fantasy creature—to stow her one crate of personal belongings in their quarters. She'd looked tired, but in good spirits, and as usual, even though fully shielded, she radiated confidence. She'd smiled when she'd greeted him and teased him about his pirate-clan look, so maybe she was on her way to forgiving him. The hope of that lessened the weight of worry he'd been carrying.

The chimes of the countdown timer sounded in his earwire and everyone else's, reminding them they only had thirty more minutes to make the liftoff window for their side of the planet. The huge *Diamantov* needed to be in the midst of the herd, or it would stand out as an easy mark for frustrated military enforcers looking to make an example.

Anitra returned unexpectedly soon, still carrying her crate. He was about to tease her about needing a guide, until he saw the stricken look on her face. He jumped off the platform and crossed to her quickly. "What's wrong?"

She set her crate down and tapped the government percomp on her arm, then pointed to her earwire. "Everyone needs to hear this."

Gavril spoke into his ship earwire. "Lizet, locate

Anitra's government band and sync it to the ship's comms."

*"Okay."* A long moment passed. *"Done."*

Anitra gestured in the percomp's interface, then spoke out loud into her earwire. "You're synced to the crew. Tell them what you told me."

*"This is Planetary Law Enforcement Chief Kareem Ferrsi. I know you have a freighter full of valuable cargo that you intend to sell to benefit the refugees. We just discovered nearly six thousand people in Lo Kuro—that's a new city on the southern continent—who were sent to a natural cave system above the city, instead of to the evacuation ships. The city's managers and council told them a big ship would be coming for them, then looted everything and lifted off in the designated evacuation ships. They went offline, presumably to hide in the crowd. We already blinded all the orbiting satellites and comms, so we don't know where they went."*

Gavril liked to think of himself as a cynic, but the widespread conspiracy needed to pull off that callous twist took his breath away.

*"We sent our only troop transport for fifteen hundred of them. If your ship can't take the rest, we'll have to send already launched ships back for as many as we can. I can send my enforcers to offload your cargo to our PLE evac ships, but it has to be now."*

The crew members he could see looked as stunned as he probably did.

Anitra cleared her throat. "Give us fifteen minutes to confer and we'll get back to you."

*"Copy that."* Ferrsi signed off.

Gavril pinged the crew. "All hands to the monster dock now." The crew on the floor started heading into the ship.

He touched Anitra's arm to stop her. "This is your project. What do you want to do?"

"Ah, hell, I don't know." She pushed escaped locks of hair out of her eyes. "I just dreamed up this crazy scheme. You and the others made it happen."

She looked so stressed that he wanted to hug her, but there wasn't time. "Let's see what the crew says."

SIXTEEN MINUTES LATER, Lizet connected Anitra's call to Ferrsi and broadcast it to the crew.

"We can take all forty-five hundred, but they'll be sleeping on supply racks. It better be a short trip to wherever we're going, because it'll be a miserable, crowded, stinky ride. And dangerous. The ship and internal systems are untested in vacuum or transit space, and we don't have escape pods or exosuits for anyone. Not enough freshers, either, and only one autodoc. One of our crew is pregnant with twins, and she and her cohab don't like their chances on the *Diamantov*, so they'll need a ride back with you and two launch berths elsewhere. That leaves us with a skeleton crew of fourteen. We're slow as a slug in atmosphere, so we'll have to go suborbital to get to the southern continent, which makes us visible. We'll be late, too. Probably the last ship off the planet."

*"We'll tell the Lo Kuro people about their options and the risks, and get them organized. Some might choose to stay*

*and take their chances, but probably not enough to make a difference. Ping me your location, and I'll send every PLE flitter and ground vehicle I can spare for the cargo. Your hard work won't go to waste."*

"Will do."

*"Thank you all,"* said Ferrsi with sincerity. *"And especially to you, Manager Helden. I'm glad we took Dammerk's word over your boss's that you belonged on the committee."* Ferrsi disconnected.

As Anitra pulled out and unfolded her tablet, Gavril raised his voice loud enough for everyone to hear. "Sinjin, Maruk, Elongo, and Nzube, tag anything we need to keep for the ship. I'll move the bus out of the way and open the dock's big bay walls so the flitters can land. Lizet, get to the nav pod and monitor comms and airlocks. Take over the repair dock's flying cameras and sync them to the shipcomp. Anitra will be on the loadmaster platform, creating new manifests for what's going and what's staying. I'll direct the load bots. I'll have to shuffle cargo so we don't lift off like a drunken elephant, so stay out of the way if you can."

The crew moved purposefully to their tasks. Gavril scooped up Anitra's crate of belongings. "I'll take this to your bunk so you can get started. What was that bit about your boss?"

She rolled her eyes. "He's a politician," she said, as if that explained everything. It probably did. "How are you holding up?"

"I'm good." He frowned. "Oh, you mean my talent. The crew is calm, so I'm okay." He blew out noisy breath. "Ask me again when we stack forty-five hundred pissed-off people onto repurposed cargo shelves and they realize we only have six freshers and no showers."

"I'll help. Don't tough it out and wait until you're overwhelmed or in blowback." She put her hand on his shoulder and massaged gently. "We need you."

## 7

* Polaris-Gamma * GDAT 3233.048 *

Anitra hated to see the last of her hoard winging its way into the hazy sky on the armored PLE flitter, but if she trusted anyone with her collection, it was solemn, intense Ferrsi. He'd arrived in person on the last PLE flitter, likely as much to assure himself the *Diamantov* was what she'd promised as to assure her he'd be an honest broker. He'd miraculously scrounged nineteen exosuits for the crew, and brought multiple crates of fresh fruits and vegetables, pre-blight grains, and cultured meats. He also brought a new volunteer crew member, his own daughter.

Salma Youssef was as tall and dark-skinned as her father, with a much more genial exterior than her gruff parent, plus ten years of law enforcement experience on Concordance planets. Her personal crate of belongings contained one change of clothing and every kind of hand weapon imaginable. Anitra sensed she was also a minder of some sort, but didn't have time to pursue it.

Anitra stood with Gavril on the platform where he operated the ship dock's console. *Déjà vu* flashed, a memory from that day two months ago when he'd played the dock's systems like a symphony conductor, wearing the same blue jacket, and turquoise braids hanging down his back. Now he was making sure the dock systems were fully detached, and wiping all records of the *Deset Diamantov* from the dock's comps. The less of a data trail, the better, if the greedy, vindictive settlement company ever sent retrievers after what they perceived as their property.

Anitra's new ship earwire sounded Lizet's tone. *"Uh, Captain? Supply Master? There's a flitter inbound, ETA two minutes. Government comms ID. The pilot said she's got some official named Minister Holtis Dalgono and seven cousins who are assigned to our ship."*

Anitra frowned as she tapped her earwire. "That's my boss. What's he... Oh, frelling hell!" She glanced down at the wide-open dock doors, then looked at Gavril. "Remember my last three finds that got jacked? I went to the supply depot yesterday to wrap things up before the evac order came down. Dalgono came by in person to tell me about a cache of mealpacks that I could take to the ship. He said, 'Too bad about the theft of the parts printers.' He's on the committee, so I figured he heard it from Ferrsi, but I just realized I didn't have time to tell anyone." She couldn't stop herself from pacing. "I kept the ship's location a secret from everyone, even Ferrsi, so I bet there's a broadcast tracer in the mealpacks. That smarmy little twist wants my farkin' ship!"

Gavril tapped his earwire. "Everyone on board, now!" He swept a hand through the holographic interface and everything went dark. "Lizet, emergency-close all the airlocks except Bravo Two. Send the flying cameras out and tell us what the flitter does. And priority-ping Chief Ferrsi and tell him what Anitra said."

Gavril took the stairs down two at a time. Anitra followed as fast as she could, but he soon outdistanced her as they headed toward the sloping ramp that would take them down to the ship. She liked wearing running boots, but hated actual running.

*"Youssef here. I'll meet you at Bravo Two with some of my toys, if someone will tell me where the hell it is."*

*"Basheer will show you. He has toys, too."* Anitra didn't know the crew's voices well enough to know who said that.

Above their heads, the tall glass walls of the ship dock vibrated in response to the low growl of a powerful flitter engine. Adrenaline coursed through her, narrowing her focus to Gavril's back.

*"They're pinging again."* Lizet sounded nervous. *"What should I say?"*

The ramp began spiraling down to arc around the *Diamantov*'s hull. She heard Gavril's out-of-breath voice in her earwire. *"Stall them."*

"Tell them," panted Anitra, "only the big freight lift is working." Glaciers moved faster than that lift.

She nearly lost sight of Gavril around the curve of

that part of the ship, and forced her aching legs to pump faster.

*"Okay."* Lizet sounded dubious.

Anitra nearly ran into Gavril, who had slowed. "Sorry."

He brushed his hand against hers. "My fault. One more ramp down." He stayed by her side until finally, they saw a big square airlock. Basheer, a strapping young man holding a beam rifle, watched behind them.

Youssef waved with a hurry-up motion. "Inside! Two mercenaries on your tail with violence on their minds."

Anitra and Gavril jumped over the threshold and into the darkened corridor of the ship. Youssef slammed the emergency seal control. The leaves of the airlock began irising inward with geriatric slowness. Anitra heard the pounding of heavy boots on the metal ramp. The sound of an energy weapon sizzled.

Basheer cursed and stumbled back. "Outer shell won't close in time."

Anitra leaned against the wall and dropped her shield. She ignored everyone but the pissed-off, determined mercs outside. She activated her strongest talent and found their visual centers, then fashioned an image of an incalloy shell dropping over the airlock as fast as on a military transport. She touched their auditory centers and shared the sound of the shell sealing tight with a pressure-release hiss and a reverberating thump. Her empath talent reported the flavor of their anger.

"Why are they stopping?" whispered Basheer.

Anitra ignored him and concentrated on the tricky part, convincing the mercs they weren't hearing the real airlock as it finally sealed. She let the mercs go. Even through the incalloy, she could feel their frustration.

Youssef turned to stared at her with narrowed, speculative eyes. "That's quite a top-level talent." Her tone held more than a hint of suspicion. "A little far from the exalted halls of the Citizen Protection Service Minder Corps, aren't you?"

"As far away as I can get." Anitra felt Gavril move closer to her, radiating protectiveness. "We didn't part on amicable terms." She moved closer to Gavril, almost touching him. She liked having someone on her side, for once.

Now that Youssef was using her mid-level sifter talent, Anitra could feel its strength. Maybe a touch of telepathy as well. She deliberately kept her shields down to indicate she wasn't hiding anything and didn't intend to fight. Sifters could detect lies, activated talents, and impending violence in others. Law enforcement agencies liked hiring sifters for interrogation teams.

"What did she do?" Basheer asked. He wasn't suspicious, just puzzled.

"Saved our asses," growled Gavril. "Lizet, status!"

*"Everything is sealed. The monster is still closing. Three mercs wearing flexin armor and a short, big-eared guy in a shiny white suit are in the little lift. Three more mercs with a bunch of big crates got in the slow freight lift. The two that were chasing you are running down the ramp. I'm trying to crack their comms encryption. Ferrsi will send the PLE as soon as he can, but that's at least an hour. Someone blew up the spaceport."*

Gavril turned to Anitra. "Can you do whatever you did again to keep them from getting in?"

"Yes." No sense keeping her secret any more, since Youssef already knew. "I'm an illusionist. Crowd-control specialist in riots and ground-conflict situations. Get me down there. Even if they get to the airlock before it closes, I can make them all hear and see that it's sealed tight."

Gavril held out his hand. "Come on. Our lifts are faster."

Anitra slipped her hand into his, grateful for his acceptance. Her talent scared people, even other minders, who believed the popular fiction stories that CPS illusionists were secretly saboteurs and assassins. She hadn't believed them until too late.

Gavril didn't let go of her hand until the lift doors opened to the cavernous hold where the monster airlock was about two-thirds closed.

*"Elongo says she froze the freight elevator with the three mercs and the gear. Big Ears and his 'cousins' are a level below."* Lizet's sneering teenage disdain made Anitra smile. *"They're pointing up the ramp toward the monster lock."*

She caught Gavril's eye. "I can't talk and hold the illusion, so if Dalgono wants to negotiate, you'll have to do it." She pointed a thumb toward the airlock. "Dalgono is vain and likes power. He's also an ideologue who detests minders."

Unexpectedly, he pulled her into a warm embrace and spoke quietly. "Do you need me for an anchor?"

She soaked in the feel of his arms around her for a long

moment, then pulled back to touch the side of his face. "Not for only eight people, but thanks for asking." She gave him a quick kiss because she couldn't resist his handsome face or the comforting flavors of affection and concern he was sending her way. She hoped they'd someday have the chance to explore that, before he returned to his trading business, and she had to pick up the pieces of her life yet again.

She regretfully pulled back and turned to face the airlock. Her illusion talent quickly found the minds of the two mercs she'd already influenced, plus the three minds below. She didn't have time to figure out which was Dalgono, because one of the two with him was a shielder. She pushed the auditory illusion of a loud airlock shell sealing at the others and delicately felt around the edges of the shield. As she'd hoped, the other minder wasn't so tightly shielded that she couldn't insinuate her talent through the shifting cracks and push the illusion. She used her empath talent on the non-shielders to give them a flavor of futility, of missing the boat. In true crowd control situations, she'd be paired with a high-level empath to give emotional depth to the sensory illusions. Done well, the combination of talents could redirect and deflate a conflict almost before it started.

Dimly, she heard voices, but blocked the distraction out. She was glad the monster airlock was nearly closed, but the incalloy in the hull made her job harder. She pushed the sound illusion of pressurized atmosphere being squeezed out as the airlock closed with an authoritative metallic clang that echoed through the dock. She pushed an illusion of silence, and a brief visual illusion of a thick incalloy shell, so the mercs would think they pictured it closed. Sometimes, the little details were the most convincing.

When the monster airlock's seal finally turned green to signal it was ready for launch, she let go of the illusions. She activated her shields as she shook her head and blinked several times to clear her mind. Her percomp told her five minutes had passed. She looked around to find only Youssef standing nearby. "How long until liftoff?"

"Ten minutes, to give the cockroaches out there time to clear, and the crew time to get the cats and dogs into their habitats." She waved toward the lift tubes behind them. "Captain wants us in the engine pod." Youssef gave her a curious look as she used the wallcomp to call the lift. "I won't ask, but someday, I hope you'll tell me your story. I bet it's ace."

"Maybe someday." She was glad Youssef seemed to have accepted she wasn't a CPS agent. She liked the tall, confident woman, and wouldn't want her for an enemy.

As they rode the lift, she wished she had a tissue for her runny nose. She'd fallen out of the habit of carrying them. She'd deliberately hidden and stopped using her illusion talent once she'd arrived on Pol-G, to reduce the chance of someone recognizing her combination of talents. She looked nothing like she had before, but deep biometrics might give her away, because she hadn't had time to get a chimera implant. Very powerful, very dangerous people thought she was dead, and she didn't want them to find out otherwise.

ANITRA LOOKED around the freighter's engine pod as she and Youssef webbed themselves into the slide-out, contoured jump seats. The pod appeared to be wrapped around a massive, spiral-shaped shiny pillar that took up most of the room. Dozens of conduits and raw cables emerged from it and vanished into the walls. A rumbling, throbbing pulse vibrated in her chest.

She dropped her shields long enough to feel Gavril's presence, and sense that he felt energized and engaged, and was successfully containing his talent.

Anitra's shipcomp earwire sparked to life.

*"Uh, Captain?"* Lizet asked. *"Minister Dalgono says if we don't give him the cargo, they'll put a hole in our hull with the flitter's wide-array beamers."*

Anitra reached through her webbing to tap Youssef's arm. "What cargo? The mealpacks?" She had to raise her voice to be heard over the engines.

Youssef rolled her eyes. "He's warped. Says he got you on the committee, so you owe him half the profit for the rich cargo. Doesn't believe we offloaded it with my father so we can rescue stranded people, even though we showed him live feeds of the empty holds."

*"Emergency liftoff protocol in sixty seconds,"* announced Gavril over the ship earwire. The rumbling pulse in the room sped up and rose in pitch. *"Lizet, replay my next words on the government channel and for the PLE."* He paused. *"Minister Dalton, you and your 'cousins' have forty-five seconds to clear or get torched by our system drive."*

Anitra looked at Youssef. "Can the beamers hurt us?"

*"Only if we sit still for twenty minutes."* That was

Gavril's voice in her earwire, because she'd forgotten to mute it when asking her question. *"Lizet and I figured it'd be a shame to let the ship dock's supply of incalloy go to waste, so we up-armored."*

Anitra smiled.

*"You should see this,"* said Lizet gleefully. *"Two of the mercs just lifted Dalgono off the ground and stuffed him in the back of the flitter with their crates."* She giggled. *"Tell her about the debris lasers and the other stuff."*

*"Later,"* Gavril responded. *"Thirty seconds to liftoff."*

Anitra snugged herself back into her jump seat. On the countless shuttles and CPS military ships she'd traveled on for her career, gravity compensators kept people from being squished when the ship pulled heavy G's through atmosphere, but who knew what the *Diamantov* had.

*"Captain,"* said Lizet. *"Flitter is clear. The merc leader took Dalgono's government percomp away from him to tell us."*

*"I'll give them an extra fifteen seconds for good behavior. Dock clamps released."*

When they lifted, the engine pod's noise assaulted her ears and the vibration threatened to rearrange her internal organs. All they had to do now was clear the twenty-story ship dock's hole in the ground and arc their way to the edge of the atmosphere. Over four thousand people in Lo Kuro were counting on them. She prayed to the constant stars the *Diamantov* and crew wouldn't let them down.

## 8

**\* Interstellar Transit Point Blockade: CGC Military Frigate "Bassilon" \* GDAT 3233.056 \***

Captain Ivar Okeanos stood at half attention, hands clasped behind him, in *Bassilon*'s executive-officer briefing room. The realtime holo conference made it seem like he stood in a crowded room of holographic ghosts of the blockade's twenty ship captains, all looking at phantom Commodore Britton on the phantom raised dais. Space Div loved technology and protocol. He kept his expression neutral but interested as Britton touched the agenda on the tablet in her hand.

"Last item. Thanks to Subcommander Paderau, *Bassilon*'s Citizen Protection Service Security Officer, we've just learned that this solar system has a second interstellar transit jump point. The main jump point we're guarding is much closer to Polaris-Gamma, so the original point was abandoned because it's inconveniently situated beyond the ringed gas giant. The coordinates haven't been published in CGC navigation updates in many years."

Paderau was undoubtedly feeling proud of herself. He'd left the information in his dataspace in an easy place for her to find. He'd had to let her overhear three increasingly blatant conversations with Sobek for her to recognize its significance and sound the alarm. He hoped it wasn't too late.

"My strategy team"—by which Britton meant the minder forecasters she illegally kept on her staff instead of forcing them to transfer to the CPS Minder Corps— "believes it's unlikely but possible that a few of the Polaris-Gamma quarantine breakers know about the old jump point and will try to use it."

Long practice kept Ivar's disgust off his face. Britton had to know the quarantine excuse was whale shit. A blight as virulent as the settlement company and the CPS claimed would have drawn a swarm of botanists and bioengineers, not a blockade-size task force of twenty well-armed military ships.

"Two days ago, the settlement company shared intelligence that the Polaris-Gamma government might be planning a mass evacuation of its population." Britton scrolled on her tablet. "Twelve hours ago, we lost all feeds from system comms and satellites, and in the last six standard hours, our active scans of the planet have detected disturbances consistent with increased ship traffic." She paused and looked up. "Therefore, I am ordering *Onilaja* and *Takala* to the far jump point." She swept the room with a sardonic gaze. "I believe the rest of us can easily prevent a hundred private yachts and merchant ships from reaching the main transit point, regardless of how quickly they scatter."

The assembled captains chuckled, as she'd intended. Ivar couldn't tell if she really believed there would only be a hundred ships instead of a thousand, or if she was giving herself cover for the inevitable internal audit inquiry into what was surely going to be a monumental clusterfuck.

*Onilaja*'s captain spoke up. "What are the rules of engagement for the second jump point?"

"Warn off, intercept, or disable." She gave everyone a diamond-hard glance. "That goes for the entire task force. No kill shots unless they come at you with military-grade weapons. These aren't jack crew or pirate clan, they're misguided civilians. We will treat them accordingly."

That unexpected directive gave Ivar hope that Britton was more savvy than he'd thought. Maybe the confrontation wouldn't be a bloodbath after all. He wondered what Paderau and the other security officers thought about that, since they were all for making Polaris-Gamma a chilling cautionary tale for other hotheaded frontier planets.

He respectfully raised his hand.

Britton pointed her chin toward him. "Okeanos, go."

"Sir, *Bassilon* is still understaffed, and our reserve flux drive is still offline. We might be better suited for the second jump point."

Britton pursed her lips a moment, then nodded. "I concur. *Onilaja* will stay here." She made a note on her tablet. "We'll send the jump point's coordinates to your nav comps so you can leave within the half hour. Use your discretion in where you deploy."

She concluded the daily briefing quickly, then dismissed them all. Ivar terminated the conference connection and touched the controls that would restore the room's usual configuration.

He'd been afraid Britton would send too many ships to the far jump point for his purposes, but now he worried that she'd sent too few. He adjusted contingencies in his plan as he strode down the corridor and into the small command pod.

Sobek vacated the command chair. "Captain."

Ivar inserted one of the command wires into the skulljack behind his ear as he turned to Sobek. "Subcaptain." Data streams began to flow into his mind. He still wasn't as facile with them as Sobek, but he was getting better. "New orders." He sent the command that let him speak to the entire crew via his earwire. "Commodore Britton is sending us and *Takala* to beyond the system's sixth planet, to enforce the quarantine at an old, disused interstellar transit jump point." He told them the rules of engagement and ordered his technical crew to collaborate with their counterparts on *Takala*, so they could leave on time.

When he was finished, he turned to Sobek, who was still standing next to him. "Going off shift?"

She nodded. "After I finish my reports."

"I don't know Chesterton. How is she to work with?" As he spoke, he flicked his eyes to Paderau, who was pretending she wasn't listening to and recording their every word.

Sobek shrugged and rubbed her nose twice. "Her second says she's regulation."

Ivar nodded. "Good. Approve the navigation plot, unless it needs my attention." He sat in the command chair and let it adapt to his contours. "I'm starting shift checks." He'd established a habit of communing with the ship's systems to read shift reports and review the ship's readiness status. He liked knowing as much as he could about his ship, and as an added bonus, it kept Paderau from trying to talk to him. She alternated between ingratiating and condescending, and challenged his ability to treat her with professional courtesy.

Sobek's nose-rubbing meant she had more to say about *Takala*'s captain, but it would have to wait until he could arrange a chance hallway encounter. Almost from his first day on the ship eleven months ago, Paderau seemed convinced it was worth her while to monitor him almost constantly. Maybe she disliked him because, like many others, she assumed he owed his present rank and command to his famous family's influence. If only.

He was pleased to discover engineering finally had the correct specifications for printing the parts needed to repair the reserve flux drive. The error hadn't been his doing, but he'd been happy to take advantage of it. Little pebbles in a pond sometimes had much bigger ripples.

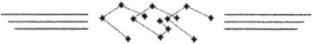

Six-point-three standard hours later, Ivar stood in front of *Bassilon*'s virtual viewport, watching the swirling gases of the giant planet in all their blue and gold glory. The colors reminded him of his youth, sailing the warm seas of his coastal home and dreaming of the stars. It had taken much longer than he'd imagined to get there.

He sent a query to the nav pod to which he already knew the answer, but needed it on the record. "How long since object geotagging has been done in this region of space?"

The navigator on duty pinged a quick reply. *"Fifty-seven years."*

"Sorry to make your life boring, but use active scans and make the geotagging a priority. We don't want any surprises because we didn't follow regulations. If you split the work with *Takala*'s nav staff, it'll go faster."

*"Yes, sir."*

Ivar set a reminder for himself to check on their progress in an hour. The task was tedious, and the crew believed *Bassilon* wouldn't be seeing any action, so they might slack off and hope he wouldn't notice.

If his necessarily convoluted plan actually worked, they'd see more action than they'd know what to do with.

He certainly hoped so.

## 9

Gavril abhorred violence, but he'd make an exception for the Lo Kuro city leaders if he ever got his hands on them. Before Ferrsi's enforcers left with the first group of refugees, they'd done their best to get the rest organized and waiting under hastily erected tents, but loading resentful adults and terrified children was a lot slower than sending load bots with crates to their assigned holds. The *Diamantov* didn't have jump seats for four thousand people, so they needed to be strapped in on the makeshift sleeping racks for liftoff.

Gavril wanted to barricade himself in the incalloy-reinforced engine pod, but if Youssef and Anitra could stand the pressure of so many minds, then so could he. No more taking the easy way out to avoid using his talent.

The modified airsled that he'd made into a loadmaster's floating platform helped him keep steady streams of people moving into the lifts and climbing the stairs and ladders. He and the crew used colored tape and cleaning bots to lead people to their assigned berths.

With only nine hundred people left to load, his talent felt a flare of angry colors somewhere outside the ship, toward the south. Sounds of shouting and scuffling ensued, implying more people were getting involved. Loading progress stopped as everyone turned back to look.

Youssef, stunner in hand, took off through the monster airlock, followed closely by a bellowing Basheer. "Make a hole!" People hastily stepped out of his way.

Anitra, who was standing below him on the cargo floor, cataloging and tagging personal goods crates, swore. "We don't have time for this."

Gavril grounded his platform next to her and held out his hand. "Get on. Let's see if we can help."

She took his hand and stepped up. He raised the platform and exited the ship into the bright, hot afternoon sunshine. He gritted his teeth against the assault of ugly emotions, but kept his talent above them, not getting lost in the seething threads. His eyes told him five or six people were swinging fists, but his talent said at least a dozen more were itching for a fight.

He moved closer to Anitra. "Tell me what to do."

She shook her head. "What happened after the restaurant was my fault. I pushed you before you were ready."

"Fine, we can share the blame and guilt later. Let's do it right this time." He took her hand in his. "Tell me what to do."

She gave him a searching glance, then nodded. "Fear and anger can fuel determination to do something. Nudge them with that. I'll give them the illusion of a sliding slope. Pump calm at anyone you can." She squeezed his hand. "Follow my talent with yours, and I'll show you."

Her shields dropped, and he felt her talent arrow toward the brawlers. He dropped his containment and went after her.

The two blood-red coils of anger that were the center of the conflict tried to snare his attention, but he avoided their threads and spread himself higher and wider. He felt Anitra's empath talent as pulses that brushed the threads and shifted them subtly toward orange and brown. He knew how to do that, so he took over that job, though it had no effect on the red-hot center.

He felt the wave of consternation from them all when Anitra's illusion hit. He took advantage of it to push more threads away from the red and into the ochre greens of action and purpose. His eyes kept wanting to flutter shut, but he forced them open, to use what his vision told him as well as his talent. Not all that different from handling input from multiple systems while piloting a ship.

The would-be brawlers were distracted and stumbling by the time Basheer and Youssef separated the primary combatants. A short, wide man with a snarl on his face took a wild swing at Youssef, who ducked it and deftly used the man's momentum and a well-timed trip to send him to his hands and knees in the dirt. She had the man's hands zip-tied behind him before he drew his next breath.

Basheer pulled the other man away into a controlling shoulder hold, talking to him in soothing tones.

Several of the nearby people still staggered around, as if chemmed, then slowly straightened up and looked at the ground suspiciously.

Gavril felt Anitra withdraw her empath talent, and he hung on to the sensation, as if he was hanging on to her sleeve, as she reeled them both in. His talent didn't want to go, but he made it cooperate. He still tanked at containment, but at least he wasn't caught in the morass this time.

He wiped the sweat off his brow with his sleeve, then focused on Anitra beside him. He realized he was still holding her hand.

She smiled. "Damn fine work, Captain."

He lifted their joined hands and kissed the back of hers. "We make a good team."

"Yes." Inexplicably, sadness flared in her before her shields shut him out. "Let's get back to our jobs so we can launch."

Thirty minutes later, he left the crew to finish loading the last group of refugees, including the two bloodied combatants, so he could get back to the engine pod for system checks.

Taking off would be clumsy. Lo Kuro didn't have an airpad big enough for a freighter, so they'd landed in a charred field of crop stubble. To speed loading, they'd landed horizontally to allow easy access to the monster airlock, but they'd have to burn more system fuel on the side jets to get the ship vertical for liftoff. The holds and lifts were on gimbals and would adjust, but the engine and nav pods were fixed. He touched his ship earwire. "Lizet, I'm at the engine pod door. Please power the grav compensator."

*"Okay. Done."*

He'd positioned himself so the local gravity pulled his feet to the floor. As he stood up, he shook his head to get his inner ear adjusted to the change. He walked around to the pilot's seat he'd rigged for himself and webbed in as he activated the wire in his skulljack and connected to the ship's systems.

*"Privet, Kapitan Danilovich."* The ship's AI greeted him in Russian because it had amused Lizet to feed it language modules in her spare time. He didn't have the heart to tell her that, despite his family name, he'd grown up speaking Hungarian, and had no one left to speak it with since his mother died twenty years ago and left him her trader ship.

He skimmed through the data streams, gratified to find few anomalies and no red flags. Through his connection, he felt the monster airlock close, and double-checked the others to ensure they read as closed. The crew would manually check them anyway, just to be sure. Nothing ruined a good flight like explosive decompression from an improperly sealed airlock.

He would have liked to top off the system drive fuel, and save flux for the interstellar transit run, but the ship had such poor atmosphere aerodynamics that they'd need the flux assist to brute-force it up and into orbit.

*"Monster lock sealed."* All the crew heard the cargo handler's announcement, and the others that followed for the rest of the airlocks. They hadn't had time to key

individual earwires to individual people, so all the crew heard all the chatter, unless they temporarily muted the earwire.

"Passenger status?" he asked.

*"They're in the holds, but not in their berths yet."* Youssef sounded exasperated. *"Maybe you could say something."*

He turned on the wired sound system they'd cobbled together, so his voice boomed throughout the ship. *"This is Captain Danilovich. This is not a farkin' pleasure cruise. You have three standard minutes to get into your assigned berths. Unless you want to find out the hard way if our one and only autodoc works, strap yourselves in now."*

*"That did it."* Youssef chuckled. *"You definitely have a way with words."*

"A gift from my mother. Grav compensators are operating in the engine pod, so you and Anitra take care at the door."

Ten minutes later, he ordered the crew to their liftoff stations.

*"On my way,"* said Anitra. *"I gave my bunk to the mother cat for liftoff."*

*"Sorry,"* said Lizet.

*"It's fine,"* replied Anitra. *"I can sleep in the engine pod's jump seat, if I have to. The pets will be good for the children."*

Gavril smiled. He'd seen her pet all the dogs and cats Lizet's elders had brought on board, so he thought the pets would be good for her, too. He'd felt her worry and sense of being overwhelmed when she'd unshielded. He wanted to tell her he greatly admired the remarkable accomplishments she'd pulled off in the midst of rampant chaos. He didn't want the whole crew to hear it, though. Their relationship was complicated enough without making a tri-D entertainment out of it.

"Powering system drives." The engines responded smoothly, filling the engine pod with their familiar vibrations. He didn't hear Youssef or Anitra enter the pod, but they both confirmed they were webbed in when he did the final crew check. Once Lizet verified the field outside was clear, he fluxed the system drives, and had the ship's AI announce a countdown throughout the ship for crew and passengers alike as he confirmed his pilot's seat web was secure.

The ride through Polaris-Gamma's atmosphere rivaled land-based thrill rides. Vaguely rectangular ships the size of a high-rise office building with token wings did not make for graceful air travel, and gravity compensators could only handle so much. Twelve bone-jarring minutes later, they cleared thermopause and passed low-orbit distance. The extra incalloy helped keep the hull temperature to well within tolerance, though the added weight cost them flux fuel for the liftoff.

"Lizet, send a narrow-beam greeting to the control ship and ask them where the hell we're going." He understood the reasons for the secrecy, but they couldn't wait any longer. As it was, they were a large, lumbering target for the blockade's military frigates. He knew one or two tricks that might get them past. The element of surprise was long gone, but if the universe loved him...

*"Uh, Captain? This is kind of weird."*

The universe hated him. "What's weird?"

*"When I sent the beam, I also pinged the CGC comms satellite for navigation chart updates, as usual. We just pulled them yesterday, so there shouldn't be any, but we just got an update. They say there's a second jump point in the system, out past Polaris-Zeta."* She made an unintelligible sound. *"It didn't used to be there. I, uh, memorized the coordinates for as many systems as I could find within transit distance. It wasn't there before."*

Gavril smiled. How very like precocious Lizet to have used her enviable minder talent for perfect recall to memorize half a galaxy's worth of transit point coordinates.

*"Might be a trap,"* suggested Youssef. *"Lure us all out to beyond the system's gas giant, so they can corral us and keep us from leaving."*

*"Too convoluted for Space Division,"* said Sinjin, Lizet's great-grandfather, the interstellar engine designer. *"They'd never mess with the nav charts. It could get them killed."*

*"The settlement company rat-bastards would do it, but they'd have to convince the military."* That was Basheer, who'd worked for Lizet's merchant family and followed them to the frontier.

*"They might only have to convince the Citizen Protection Service,"* said Anitra. *"The CPS has agents on any military ship of size."*

*"Huh?"* asked Lizet, echoing Gavril's own confusion. *"Why would the CPS care?"*

*"Because,"* replied Anitra, *"Polaris-Gamma repeatedly told the CPS to suck flux. No clinics, no minder-testing centers, no representatives, no Jumper bases, no remands of*

*fugitives, not even of minders."* Her voice sounded tired. *"Pol-G is a bad influence. Might inspire other frontier planets to do the same."*

*"That's what my father says, too,"* chimed in Youssef.

Gavril stretched his shoulders, trying to loosen the tension. "Lizet, find out what's happening with the rest of our fleet. We're on the planet's dark side from the blockade for the moment, but not for long." The active pings against the *Diamantov*'s abundant sensors felt like echoes, not recent.

*"When I sent the cryptogon key Chief Ferrsi gave us, we got a message,"* said Lizet.

"Share it with the crew," ordered Gavril. "We're late to the party."

Ferrsi's distinctive, precise diction sounded in his earwire. *"If you haven't already done so since this morning, update your nav charts from the CGC, then check for a second jump point, past Polaris-Zeta. Two-thirds of our ships are headed for it. The rest decided to take their chances at the known jump point. If you have any weapons, don't shoot at the blockade unless you have no choice. Your assigned destination is Sivari Intalo, a frontier planet eight transit days from here. They've agreed to act as a clearinghouse for your passengers. Good luck to you all."*

Youssef spoke up. *"My father believes the new jump point is legit, or he'd have said something."*

"All in favor," said Gavril, "of not getting our asses shot off at the main blockade, say 'aye.'" A full chorus of "ayes" from the crew resounded in his ear. "Lizet, plot a high-and-wide arc over the system's elliptic. We'll take a curving shot at that jump point and use a gravity assist from the gas giant's big fat moon. With luck, we'll avoid any traffic in the more conventional approach."

Minutes later, he used his connection to the ship to send the commands for a smooth and steady acceleration on Lizet's nav solution. He was deeply gratified that all their hard work had transformed the *Diamantov* into their best shot for finding a new home.

At some point in the last few days, or maybe even before that, he'd come to think of himself as one of the team. He liked the feeling of being a part of something. He'd used his solo trader career to protect himself from getting hurt through his empath talent, and told himself he was a loner, but he'd been hiding. Cowering, really. Letting the fear of his talent and the fear of rejection keep him on the outside, only occasionally stepping in from the cold when loneliness got too much to bear. Two years ago, Anitra had offered the promise of something better, but he'd been too stubborn to realize it.

Even though he'd stupidly ruined his chances with her, it had been an easy decision to pilot the *Diamantov* to benefit her people. In a way, his people, too. He'd become interwoven with their emotional presence, even if he only personally knew the crew.

He sent a bit of his talent out to the nearest crew members, to check that they were all right. Skittish, brilliant Lizet was scared, but even more exhilarated. Youssef felt almost bored, but with an undercurrent of blended wariness and anticipation that he'd noticed in law enforcers, the kind her father had in spades.

He lingered the longest on the oasis of nothingness that was Anitra, wishing for once he could connect his empath talent with hers. They'd done it briefly, after quelling the would-be brawl in Lo Kuro, and he wanted to explore that again with her. Even more than he wanted her in his bed, he wanted that connection.

He unwebbed himself from the pilot seat and got to his feet, stretching the tension out of his back. He set the holo console the way he liked it, with visual representations of their progress and the planets they'd pass, then walked around the engine core to the jump seats.

Youssef was already striding through the open engine pod doorway. "There ought to be a law that all engine pods must have freshers." She raised her voice in the corridor. "Damn vibrations tickle my bladder."

He turned to share his amusement with Anitra, but she was fast asleep in her jump seat. He crouched beside her and checked that her webbing was secure. Usually in sleep, she just looked relaxed, but faint bruising under her eyes hinted at deep exhaustion. He smoothed her hair back off her face, taking comfort in the warmth of her skin and the surprising softness of her wavy hair.

She'd made everything they'd accomplished possible, but he doubted she'd see it that way. She probably thought it was simply the right thing to do, not realizing that most people would have given it up as impossible from the start. Her true gift was sharing her vision, inspiring people to do whatever it took to make it real. He wished he knew what she wanted for herself, because he'd like to be the one to give it to her.

He snorted to himself as he stood. First, they had to make it past the blockade.

## 10

**\* Interstellar Transit Point Near Polaris-Zeta:
Freighter "Deset Diamantov" \* GDAT 3233.049 \***

With no ship crew responsibilities for the five hours it would take to get to Polaris-Zeta, and no more ramper chems to keep her wired, Anitra dozed off in the engine pod's jump seat. The next she knew, someone was nudging her.

She opened her eyes to see Gavril wearing his favorite blue jacket, even though the engine pod bordered on hot. His serious expression alarmed her. She unwebbed and sat forward on the edge of the seat, hoping she hadn't been snoring louder than the engines.

He sat sideways in the other jump seat. "You should hear this." He pointed to the earwire that had fallen onto her chest.

She re-adhered it to her jaw. "*...repeat, this is the Concordance Command Peace Frigate* Bassilon. *This system is under quarantine. Stand down and identify your* *ship.*" The mid-range voice was gender-neutral, but a real human, and had a Mandarin accent.

"What's going on?" She freed her hair and ran her fingers through it, then replaced the two combs.

"From what we can piece together from comms and pings, two-thirds of the Pol-G refugee ships chose the far jump point at Pol-Zeta, like we did. Only two Space Div frigates guarded it, and although they ordered the ships to turn back and painted them with weapons pings, they didn't shoot. The refugee ships just navigated around them and jumped. That was maybe six hundred ships in about four hours, because the Pol-G controller sent them in waves. I figure the last of them went through right as we cleared Pol-G's thermosphere." He shook his head. "We're giving a whole new meaning to 'fashionably late.'"

"Okay, what's the bad news?"

"It didn't go so well at the main jump point. Eighteen Space Div frigates formed a moving sphere to protect the jump coordinates. Maybe fifty Pol-G ships got by them, but that still left incoming waves of three hundred ships. It was a standoff, until something bad happened, and all of a sudden, we're getting pings that some of the frigates were shooting, and people were dying." Gavril stood and held out his hand. She took it and let him help her get to her feet. Gravity felt normal, but her stomach bottomed out, probably because she hadn't eaten anything since... she couldn't remember when.

"About thirty minutes after we launched, CGC comms went dark. I kept us on course for the Zeta jump point, but now we have trouble." He motioned her to follow him around the thrumming engine core to his pilot station. He pointed to a holo display depicting space. "This shows our realtime active scan results. Those red icons are four military frigates. The yellow diamond is us. The blue dots are the jump-point safety zone." The red icons moved in a complex, stuttering pattern just outside the blue dots. "If we were faster and smaller, we could slip in between their perimeter."

The synthvoice of the *Diamantov*'s shipcomp spoke in their earwires. *"Active scans detected. Target pings detected. Target solutions achievable from Red One, Red Two, Red Three, Red Four."*

She was no spacer, but "target solutions" sounded like a bad thing.

Gavril crossed his arms as he spoke out loud. She heard it in her earwire, too, meaning so did the crew. "Peace Frigate *Bassilon*, this is Captain Danilovich of the freighter *Deset Diamantov*. We have four thousand and twelve adults and children, and eight newborn kittens. We aren't looking for trouble. All any of us are looking for is a new home." Gavril sounded marvelously calm.

The ship's synthvoice spoke again. *"Active scans detected."*

Worry coursed through her. "Shouldn't you have Youssef or someone with tactical experience in here with you?" She stepped back. She was out of her depth, and likely in the way. Gavril moved closer.

He pointed to his earwire. "They're already online." He brushed a stray lock of hair off her forehead. "You needed the sleep, but now I need to know how Space Div ships operate, how they think. None of our crew has that kind of experience, and I don't want to scare the passengers by asking them." He gave her a brief smile. "My talent says they're mostly calm right now, and I'd prefer they stay that way."

She gave him an exasperated look. "Oh, thanks, no pressure." She thought back to the few times she'd been on a Space Div ship involved in an enforcement action. "The blockade enforcers haven't killed anyone—before today, that is—but they have confiscated ships. Some frigates are big enough to carry dozens of smaller ships like pinnaces or patrollers. They always have a temporary leader if it's three or more ships together. Most of the captains I knew were steady and conservative, and would need a good reason to fire on unarmed refugee ships." She frowned. "Spacers, at least the rankers, can be hotheaded. If some equally hotheaded settlers tried to shoot their way past the blockade..." She shrugged.

*Bassilon*'s Mandarin-accented comms person came online. "*Deset Diamantov, your configuration is a Leidari-class freighter, but with three times the armor. What weapons do you carry?*" The query's tone hinted at suspicion.

Gavril called up a holo image of the *Diamantov* as he responded. "None, unless you count debris lasers." He highlighted twelve places on the ship's hull, then whisked away with a flick of his finger. "See for yourself."

He touched his earwire, meaning he spoke to the crew. "I sent *Bassilon* the *Diamantov*'s diagram with our lasers, but not the power rating, or the sensors and scanners."

"What sensors and scanners?" asked Anitra, leaving her earwire on so the crew would hear her question.

He smiled. "Along with the extra incalloy, the repair dock had spare parts in storage. We were going to add them to your cargo for sale, but Lizet and I decided we may as well get use out of them for the trip." He waved toward the console. "I didn't think about it making us look like we're jackers masquerading as a merchant ship." His mouth tightened. "All crew should probably be in exosuits, in case things go down twisted. Lizet, you especially. Leave them open for now, but ready to seal."

He pointed to a cabinet on the far wall, which she opened to find three exosuits hanging on hooks. She took out the tall and short one, leaving the middle-sized one for Youssef, in case she came back. Gavril had to take off his jacket to get the exosuit over his broad shoulders, then had to show her how to seal hers and explain how the plumbing worked. She'd never had occasion to wear one.

*Bassilon*'s next communication came from a different voice, a woman's, with a slight German accent. *"We have reason to believe you have no passengers, and are instead smuggling high-value goods looted from Polaris-Gamma and blight-infected plant material. Prepare to be boarded and inspected."*

"Negative," snapped Gavril. "None of our airlocks are space-rated. I don't know where you got your information, but our cargo is people."

Gavril looked like he wanted to pace, so she moved back to give him room. The injustice of the accusation infuriated her.

A complex mix of anger and sadness flitted across Gavril's face as he turned away from her. He rolled his shoulders and tilted his head from side to side. "Lizet, put a synchronized timestamp on the flying cameras in the passenger holds and send me twenty seconds of raw vid with audio."

Anitra knew she should be at the cargo master's console, or the galley, where she'd be more useful. Selfishly, she'd wanted to stay with Gavril because he made her feel safe, but the whole ship depended on him. She reluctantly took a step toward the exit.

*"Vids in your dataspace."* Lizet sounded tense, but calm. *"I sent other cameras to the supply holds, but it'll take a few minutes."*

"Good thinking." Gavril manipulated something in the holo interface. *"Bassilon*, sending you a tight-beam packet with realtime vids of our passengers." He emphasized the last word. "Lizet, you're our resident math genius. Look for an exploitable opening in the frigate flight patterns that puts us in transit the millisecond we're in the jump zone. As big and slow to accelerate as we are, we'll only have one shot."

He turned to look at Anitra, but addressed the whole crew via his earwire. "For those of you who can't access the shipcomp right now, I'll tell you what it says. Avoiding the frigates will cost us time and flux that I'd rather save for when we get to Sivari Intalo, but it's either that, or stay here and play tag with four of Space Div's finest. Anyone with better tactical ideas, speak up."

Ever since Anitra heard the name of their destination, she felt like she'd forgotten something important about it, and it finally bubbled to the surface. "The CPS has a big field office and Jumper base on Sivari," she told Gavril and the crew. "CPS security officers have private comms outside Space Div's network. We can't tell the *Bassilon* where we're going, or we'll have a welcoming committee."

Gavril blew out an explosive breath that could be heard over the earwire. "The universe fucking hates me." He rotated the holo showing the frigates in motion. "Lizet, find us a jump that's three or four transit days from here, where we can take on flux if we need to."

Her answer came back immediately. *"I've got three. Pol-G used to sell surplus flux on J'Letha, four days away. My family had the shipping contract. Want me to queue it as an alternative?"*

"Add them all," said Gavril. "I'm sending your vids of the holds to *Bassilon*."

Anitra found she'd somehow moved closer to Gavril again. Dammit. She muted her earwire. "I'm going to the fresher and to the–"

She was interrupted by a new ping from *Bassilon*. *"Captain Danilovich,"* said the German-accented woman, *"perhaps you are unaware that one of your passengers is former Supply Depot Manager Anitra Sando Helden, who is subject to a detain-and-restrain order from Polaris-Gamma for grand larceny, destruction of government property, and kidnapping. She is also a multi-talent minder."*

Anitra frowned. "What the hell?" Nothing like stirring up a little bigotry to make non-minders view her as dangerous.

Gavril shook his head disgustedly as he keyed the comm to the *Bassilon*. "Apparently," he said acidly, "I'm also unaware that the CGC military has added nonmember frontier-planet law enforcement to their mission."

The ensuing silence encouraged her, though perhaps it shouldn't have. Out beyond the borders of civilized space, jurisdictional violations would be hard to prove.

*"Captain,"* said Lizet. *"I sent three solutions to get through their pattern. Two straight runs that put us within laser distance of one of their frigates. The third takes two vector changes and depends on them not seeing the flaw in their pattern in time to fix it."*

Gavril enlarged the holo display to show the three solutions side by side.

Youssef pinged. *"How did the* Bassilon *know Helden is on board? Or for that matter, what our ship used to carry?"*

*"Settlement company spies?"* asked Lizet.

Realization hit Anitra. She tapped her ship earwire. "Yes, and specifically, Dalgono." She muttered a vile epithet. "Ten to one, he was playing both sides for maximum self-enrichment. Wouldn't surprise me if he forced the committee's hand into launching on his schedule. When we repelled him and his mercenary cousins, I bet he told the settlement company, who told the military, because he still wants my farking ship."

*"Who were you supposed to have kidnapped?"* asked Lizet.

"The whole crew, probably." Another realization tumbled into place. "Gavril, I think the German woman might be the *Bassilon*'s CPS security officer. The military doesn't play games like this. She's trying to distract or delay you."

*"Or provoke you,"* suggested Youssef, *"so they can claim self-defense."*

Gavril enlarged the holo display to a full meter's size. "Lizet, plot a hybrid solution that looks like we're going for one of your straight runs, but at the last possible minute, overload flux for the two-vector solution that hits their pattern flaw. Use the best speed that leaves us thirty-percent flux reserves."

*"What's our interstellar transit destination?"*

"J'Letha." He touched a control on the console. "*Bassilon*, we don't want trouble, but four thousand people are depending on us to get them to safety, and we don't have enough flux to wait for you to decide. You obviously let all the other ships go before us. Are you really going to shoot the last one?"

*"Solution plotted on your holo,"* said Lizet.

Gavril rotated the holo. New lines and symbols appeared. "Good. Execute in fifteen seconds." He brought up a second display that Anitra didn't recognize. "Come on, *Bassilon*," he muttered, "ask me."

Anitra thought if she'd played more war games as a teen, she might have a clue about Gavril's tactics. She'd once again drifted closer, like he was a subtle whirlpool that drew her in.

Enough. She was useless there, and a distraction. She waved to catch his attention and muted her ship's earwire. "I need a fresher and food." She pointed toward the exit.

He nodded. "Stay connected. I don't want to lose you." He pointed to her earwire, but the words felt weightier, more emotional than that. She searched his serious expression, tempted to drop her shield and find out.

"Deset Diamantov, *what is your destination?*" The Mandarin-accented voice was back.

"Yes!" Gavril smiled and fist-bumped the air. He touched the comms control. "*Bassilon*, we're going to J'Letha. Here's my chart."

He flicked something in the interface, then tapped his earwire for the crew to hear. "Lizet, show us all a countdown clock for the upcoming course change." The holo display behind him showed nine minutes and decreasing seconds. "I sent Space Div our J'Letha nav solution, and accidentally-on-purpose included our straight-line path through the blockade. I hope it makes them complacent enough not to active-scan us until we get within energy-weapons range. By which time, we'll be burning flux toward Lizet's hole in the fence."

*"Should Helden and I be with the passengers when we do all these vector changes?"* asked Youssef. *"We haven't told them jack about any of this."*

"No, the grav compensators will..." He trailed off. "Actually, yeah, but for the jump to transit. Should be smooth, but some children are sensitive to it, like cats and dogs."

Anitra smiled, glad for something useful she could do. She knew absolute zero about piloting ships or outsmarting Space Div frigates. Crowds, she could handle.

## 11

**\* Interstellar Transit Point Near Polaris-Zeta:
Freighter "Deset Diamantov" \* GDAT 3233.050 \***

Gavril paced back and forth in the only pattern the cramped engine pod allowed. The engines thrummed with power and vibrated the marrow of his bones. He heard the shipcomp's AI announce the five-minute warning for entry into interstellar transit space.

The wire in his skulljack allowed him to feel when two of the misbegotten Space Div pinnaces crossed his forward path close enough to count their gunports. He'd already designated them as Pin 1 and Pin 2 for the visual holo plot, to help track them. The frigates had discovered his vector changes too late to block him, but their unbelievably fast and agile pinnaces were doing their damnedest to make the *Diamantov* slow down or veer off. Pin 3 paralleled their flight and took periodic pulse-beamer shots at his sensors, trying to blind him on one side.

His constant active-scans told him when two more pinnaces joined the fray and began using cutting lasers on the freighter's airlocks and engine ports, just like jackers trying to slice open a fat merchant ship. Through his interface, he felt the hull heat.

He couldn't shoot back, or the mother frigate would pound the *Diamantov* to atoms, but he didn't have to make their jobs easy.

"Lizet, I'm rolling us on X axis for the last three minutes. Shouldn't affect transit entry, but watch for bubble anomalies, once we're in." He sent the commands to the trim jets and engine ports that started the *Diamantov* spinning. The pinnaces would have to roll with him to make accurate shots with lasers or pulse beamers.

Pin 1 and Pin 2 circled around for another harrying maneuver. Pin 1 zoomed ahead, twisting on an angle, closer to the *Diamantov* than ever. Pin 2 mirrored the flight path, but neglected the twist, putting it on a collision path with *Diamantov*'s bulky wing cover.

Gavril ordered the *Diamantov* to spin faster and shouted into the broadbeam comm. "Turn, you lopar! Turn!"

Pin 2 turned a second later, but it was too late. Its wing tangled with *Diamantov*'s. The freighter's mass and extra incalloy won. The pinnace's wing tore off and sent the rest tumbling like a toy.

Gavril sent another broad-beam comm. "*Bassilon* and whoever else is listening, you've got a pinnace pilot eating hard space. Sending scan readings for last known vector." It was the best he could do for them.

*"Two minutes until transit,"* announced the calm synthvoice of the shipcomp's AI.

The sensors said *Diamantov*'s wing cover was shredded, and the ship's AI reported it as unresponsive.

Pin 1 veered wide in the direction of Pin 2's mortally wounded ship. The other three pinnaces continued the parallel flight paths, but at a safer distance.

*"Deset Diamantov, you are now subject to detainment for destruction of military property and attempted murder."* The German-accented voice sounded subtly triumphant. *"We will commence disabling fire unless you decelerate immediately."*

Gavril tapped the ship earwire. "Emergency transit entrance in thirty seconds."

*"But we're outside the zone,"* said Lizet.

"Better that than being slagged by Space Div." He made the ship's AI announce the fast transit warning. "We've lost a wing cover. Our entrance might be rocky. All crew, seal exosuits." He followed his own orders and sealed his. Better uncomfortable than dead.

He engaged the flux drive and watched the internal readouts closely. All dock tests had declared the drive fully operational, but going transit was the only test that mattered.

At ten seconds before transit, he sent a broadbeam comm to Space Div. *"Deset Diamantov* respectfully declines your invitation for tea and crumpets. Another time, perhaps."

The transition to transit space went smoothly, except for the shards of incalloy they undoubtedly left in the realspace at Polaris Zeta.

After ten minutes of steady, quiet operation in transit and no system alerts anywhere, Gavril relaxed his vigilance enough to make an announcement to the crew. "You can unseal exosuits. All hands to the galley in fifteen minutes."

THE *DIAMANTOV*'S newly remodeled galley strained to hold fifteen people, four purebred Thunderbolt shepherds, and one muscular, bobtailed, tufted-eared cat that kept pouncing on the cleaning bots.

Gavril deliberately activated his talent long enough to make sure everyone was all right. Youssef was tightly contained, probably a result of dealing with the passengers. Anitra was the usual oasis of nothingness, but she smiled and gave him a slight nod of approval. Lizet kept her head down, refusing to look at anyone, but her colors were more wary than afraid.

"I'll want to hear about the passengers in a minute, but first, we have to talk about where we're going." He started to shove his hands in his pockets, but the exosuit didn't have any. He settled for hooking his thumbs through the tool loops. "I probably shouldn't have tweaked Space Div's noses with my last comm, but I'll bet my share of the onboard ale that they ordered a squadron to meet us at J'Letha the moment I sent our itinerary. Which is why I propose to bend transit space and send us to Sivari Intalo."

Lizet looked up, startled. "We can *do* that?"

"Yes, dear." Sinjin, Lizet's elder, patted her hand. "It's

why he had you keep the thirty-percent reserve of flux in your nav plots."

Gavril nodded. "No matter how well we schedule our limited resources, it'll mean eight increasingly uncomfortable days for our passengers. Those of you who have spent time with them, tell me now if you think they can't handle it."

Elongo spoke first. "Twelve have already told me about health issues, and I'd put another thirty or so on the watch list, mostly for addictions. With four thousand people, we're guaranteed to have more. The good news is we have five trained healers in the group who volunteered their services. Not everyone will agree to be treated by a minder, but that's their problem."

Youssef stood up from her slouch against the restaurant-sized cold box. "For those of you who don't know, I'm a sifter and a low-level telepath. No one's feeling violent right now, but that'll change once they get sick of mealpacks and sick of their neighbors, with no way to blow off steam. We need an exercise room and maybe a sparring arena. We'll also need some isolated spaces for people who can't handle crowds." She frowned. "The Citizen Protection Service's official line is that fifteen percent of the galaxy's population are minders, but anyone in law enforcement knows it's more like thirty or forty percent. And even higher on Polaris-G, because word got around that they told the CPS to bugger off. When tempers flare, it's easy to blame minders for any trouble." She crossed her arms. "I can usually tell who's a minder and who isn't, but I won't have any part of treating minders differently from non-minders. That separate-justice, assumption-of-guilt bullshit is why my family moved out of the Concordance to the frontier in the first place."

Gavril felt some threads of discomfort arise in some of the crew, but no one seemed outraged, or even challenged, by Youssef's declaration. It probably helped that they'd hired the crew from personal referrals, rather than out of the spaceport job lists. He turned to look at Anitra when she cleared her throat.

"I'm a shielder and a low-level empath... and an illusionist. I was CPS-trained as a crowd-control specialist, but I like teaching better. If we have minders who are just coming into their talents and don't know what's happening, I can help. The mood of the passengers is surprisingly good, considering they were royally screwed by people they trusted, then shoved onto glorified bread racks in five freighter holds." She waved toward Youssef. "Salma is right about needing more space for quiet time and exercise. We'll need a playroom, too. Nothing like cranky kids to give everyone in hearing distance a headache."

"Our dogs can help," offered Sinjin. "We breed them for companionship. They're good for calming people down and playing with the children."

Cargo Handler Y'Nah raised a hand. "If we ask for volunteers, I bet we get help to fix up more of the holds. Give 'em room to spread out." Her unidentifiable polyglot accent suggested a childhood on the mean streets of a megacity. Most older planets in the Concordance had at least one. "Give 'em something to do 'sides count the bulkhead seams. Settlers ain't good at sitting on their asses."

Anitra snapped her fingers. "We've still got that flat storage area full of bond paints that were used to paint the monster airlock. I could teach art classes. If we can make the little holds habitable first, we could ask for volunteer teachers in other subjects, too."

"We need an activity director, or it'll be chaos," said Elongo. "Can't be any of us. We've got a ship to run."

Gavril nodded. "Let's ask the passengers for volunteers. We should tell them what's happening, too. We don't want to be like the shithead city managers who lied to them."

They spent another twenty minutes making shift schedules for duties, meals, and sleeping, and making a prioritized list of habitation projects. As individual crew members, they had very little in common except their shared history on Polaris-G and a shared purpose of escaping it, but it seemed to be enough to make them into a team.

"Come on, Lizet. I'll teach you how to bend space." He leaned in conspiratorially. "Don't tell your parents who taught you. I like living."

Sinjin and his husband Maruk laughed. "We're old and deaf," said Sinjin. "We didn't hear anything."

"Eh?" said Maruk.

Lizet giggled.

EIGHT HOURS LATER, Gavril found Anitra in their shared quarters, reading her tablet. And serving as a snuggle pad for a couple of the two-week-old kittens from the open yellow habitat that took up half her bed. The kittens' eyes had just opened the day before, but they were still wobbly, warmth-seeking bundles of spotted brown fur with striped heads. She wore shorts and a loose, paint-spattered top, and looked more comfortable and relaxed than he'd seen her in weeks. She gave him a wide smile when he came in. "Is Lizet now an honorary member of the pirate clan?"

Gavril chuckled. "Yeah, she's in bliss. I just know the technique. She's trying to work out the math for it."

"Good. I get the impression she hasn't been allowed to shine."

He took off his coat and hung it by the door. "Where did you put your exosuit?" He waved his hand over the control that unfolded his bed.

"Fresher." She tilted her chin toward the sliding door. "I installed extra hooks, in case you wanted to air yours out for a bit. Mine got pretty rank, and I only wore it for a few hours. I ran its cleaning cycle."

He looked down at his waist, where his belt kept his suit half on, hanging down the back. "As the on-call pilot, I should wear it at all times, but to hell with it. I don't want people to smell me coming down the hall."

He pulled off the exosuit and found the cleaning controls, then carried it to the fresher and put it on the hook next to Anitra's. Seeing the tiny built-in clothes sanitizer inspired him to strip off his sweaty pants, shirt, and underwear and put them in it. He stepped into the chemical mist shower and rubbed himself down. As captain, he could have exempted himself from the no-water-for-showers rule, but he wasn't better than anyone else, just lucky to be the person Anitra thought of when she found the ship.

He wrapped a towel around his hips and went back to his bed and sat. Without the stim drugs, he should be dead on his feet, but he still felt wide awake. He wasn't used to sharing a room, either. He cautiously sent a thread of talent toward Anitra. He encountered her shields, as expected, but they seemed more porous than usual, with shades of emotion almost visible. A mix of inspiration and worry, maybe. "What are you reading?"

"Recipes." She made a holo of a pot of stew appear. "We don't have a stasis box, so the fresh fruits and vegetables Ferrsi gave us will only last a week in the cold box. They'll last longer if I cook them into things now and freeze them for later."

One of the kittens on her lap began to mew piteously, so she put both of them back in the habitat, then gave the mother cat soft strokes and murmured praise as she checked the habitat's food and water supplies.

"You don't mind cooking for the crew?" She'd volunteered during the first meeting and had already cooked two meals and made a variety of snacks.

"I like being useful, and to use Salma's phrase, I don't know jack about running a ship." She sat on her bed again, next to her tablet. "That reminds me. How hard would it be to change the name of the ship?"

"Middling hard. The name is easy, because that's just a convenience, but the unique registration ID is squirreled away everywhere. Lizet knows the shipcomp better than I do."

"Salma and I think it might help us slip under the scanners before the CPS at Sivari Intalo notices. Since your bend-space trick means we can't drop into realspace to pick up comms packet updates, we're flying in blind. A lot can happen in eight transit days."

"Good point." He should have thought of it himself. Maybe he wasn't as alert as he imagined. He dropped his chin to his chest to stretch out his neck muscles. He needed a massage.

"I'm going to need a new name, too."

Her words were matter of fact, but a thread of forlorn dull green leaked from her shields. He looked up. "Because of the phony detain warrant for you on Pol-G?"

"Yeah, that, plus... " She sighed. "Once upon a time, an idealistic young woman with multiple minder talents graduated from the prestigious CPS Minder Institute and was proud to accept what she thought was a needed-service job with the CPS Minder Corps. She stopped countless people from getting hurt, stopped cities from burning. And when she wasn't using her talents, she trained others how to use theirs."

He cautiously activated more of his talent. Her shields leaked threads of guilt and a deep sense of betrayal. He wanted to comfort her, but was afraid he'd derail her story.

"She stupidly, stubbornly disbelieved the rumors about what people like her did with their talents, and refused to see the pattern of unfortunate civilian deaths that coincided with her team's deployments." She slid a small pillow onto her lap. "This woman fell in love with a man outside the service, but the relationship was strained by his attempts to get her to see the truth. To prove him wrong, she monitored traffic in a key office, sure she'd find nothing. When the facts proved her cohab right, she monitored other comms, convinced it was just one bad outlier. It wasn't." She toyed with the pillow's tasseled corner. Her shields were barely containing her sense of loss. Gavril clasped his hands together to keep from reaching for her and distracting her.

"Long story short, she gave all her evidence to the Office of Internal Investigation and a famous journalist, faked her own death, got a makeover, and paid the settlement price on the frontier planet with the least contact with the CPS she could find. It took her three months to recover from enhancement drug withdrawal. The ex-cohab she left behind and the journalist are dead. If the CPS catches her, she will be, too." She pulled the pillow up and cradled it against her stomach. "So, I need a new name. Again."

She shook her head once, then set the pillow aside and squared her shoulders. He felt the indigo-colored resolve brush aside the charcoal threads of loneliness and isolation. He marveled at her strength of will. "I'm keeping you from sleeping, and the ship needs you well-rested." She pushed to her feet. "I'll go check on the galley."

"Please stay." Gavril patted the bed beside him, then held out his hand. When she hesitated, he added, "This clever woman I know said empaths like you and me need physical contact."

A corner of her mouth lifted in amusement. "Oh, yeah, it's for our health."

"I don't mean sex. Not that I don't want you, because I do, every time I see you, but my talent says you're hurting right now. Let me help."

She hesitated a moment more, then put her hand in his. He gently reeled her in to sit beside him, and snuggled her under his arm. He felt her shields thin, but they were still there. He set his containment free to enjoy the muted texture of her emotions and share his. "I'd like to earn your trust again."

She turned to look at him. "What are you talking about? I trust you."

"Not with my talent, you don't." He shook his head. "And you shouldn't. I don't trust me, either. I hurt you."

"Once, and not maliciously. I hurt you, too, by pushing too hard. You'd learned more in two months than others take years to learn, and I forgot you're still a beginner." She slid out from under his arm to face him more fully, taking his hand in hers. "We both hurt and got hurt. Let's try not to do it to each other again."

She put her hand on his towel-covered thigh, and with that, her shields melted away. Her talent and emotions rose to mingle with his. He'd never felt anything like it. She was a compelling, complex tapestry of moving colors and threads, vibrating with an energy he had no words to describe. He held nothing back from her.

He cradled her face in his hands and kissed her once, then a second time, because she tasted so good. She slid herself into his lap and kissed him back as if she were an explorer on a sensuous expedition. His talent felt her rising passion, and he couldn't have hidden his body's response to her if he'd wanted to.

"You are always," she said between kisses that trailed along his jaw, "the sexiest man in the room."

He chuckled "I'm the only man in the room." He glided one hand up the contour of her hip to slip under her top and stroke the skin of her stomach. She found his earlobe with her lips. Her soft gasp of pleasure into his ear raised goosebumps on his arms, despite the warmth of their quarters. He reluctantly pulled back to look at her strong, beautiful face. "I didn't mean to take advantage of you while you're vulnerable. Sex with you is amazing, but last time, we let it stop us from talking."

She flattened her palm on his chest. "What does your talent tell you?"

"That right now, you want this as much as I do." He brushed a thumb across her cheek. "But emotions are ephemeral, driven by thought, and I'm no telepath. I don't want to break your heart, and I don't want you to break mine."

Tears formed in her eyes, and one dropped. Because of their connection, he knew she wasn't sad or angry. She slid her hand up to his shoulder. "I've tried to picture making a quiet living somewhere on Sivari Intalo, but the presence of that CPS base worries me. My shields aren't strong enough to keep a high-level telepath from discovering the secrets I carry." She shook her head. "I truly believed the Citizen Protection Service was a good organization, and offered a safe haven for minders in a galaxy that hates us. Now I'm afraid of it." Threads of betrayal and resentment surfaced in her, then subsided. She wiped away the tear. "What do you want?"

He took a deep breath and let it out slowly. "You," he said bluntly. "I was thinking of claiming to be a Pol-G refugee so Sivari would let me settle with you."

That startled her. "But you love your trader career... your ship."

"I do, but not as much as I love you." He brushed her soft hair back off her face. "You knew that from the moment you dropped your shield, but words are important."

"Yes, they are." Another tear fell. "I love you, too." She gave him a trembling smile. "You may as well get used to the waterworks. I'm a crier."

"I don't mind, as long as you don't shut me out." He kissed her forehead. "I know you can't go around unshielded, but you can still tell me what's going on."

"I'll try." She tapped his chin with her finger. "You, too. You liked living alone."

He shook his head. "I didn't. I told myself I didn't like people, but it was just people in crowds I couldn't handle. I missed having friends." He sent her a mental caress of love. "I missed you a lot after we broke up."

She tilted her head, a speculative look on her face.

He felt the energy of creativity rise to her surface. "You have an idea."

"Is the offer to come with you on your ship still open?"

"Yes, but the trader's life would be a waste of your considerable skills and experience. And you like people. That's why I was thinking of becoming a settler."

"My first thought about a new career was to become a cook, but now, I'm thinking of becoming a teacher. I'd advertise art classes, but I'd also like to quietly teach people like you to use their minder talents, without involving the CPS." Her eyes took on the faraway look she got when she was envisioning possibilities. "I have funds... well, anonymous cashflow chips, to buy into your business. We could trade a little, teach a little, and see if we can find a place in the galaxy that suits us." She twitched an eyebrow at him. "Since my family, such as it is, thinks I'm dead, you can introduce me to the pirate clan side of your family."

He chuckled. "I'd have to introduce myself first. My parents split when I was five, and when I was fourteen, we got the news my father had died. My mother gave me his vest, but refused to tell me anything about him or his clan. I romanticized them as a kid."

"Understandable. I wanted to be an exploration spacer." She snorted. "Then I met some of them, and they're worse than CPS Institute graduates for their sense of entitlement."

He kissed her nose. "Even worse than pilots?"

"Pilots aren't arrogant, they're just crazy." She trailed delicate fingers down his chest. "How long until you have to go back on shift?"

"Hours." He tilted up her chin and kissed her until they both were shuddering with desire. "Hours and hours."

## 12

* Frontier Planet "Sivari Intalo" * GDAT 3233.068 *

Anitra, or Norika Deo, as she was known in the
official refugee lists, sat on a soft, plush lounge
chair in the common area of the *Corviniana*, Gavril's
trader ship, sipping a cup of hot chocolate. She watched
with amusement as Gavril and Lizet's fifteen-year-old
cousin Tamazo took Lizet on a tour of the ship. Tamazo, a
slender, pale-skinned boy with glowing gold and red hair
that made him look like a solar collector, took nearly as
much pride as Gavril in showing off the ship's combined
engine and nav pod. Ever since Lizet had shown Tamazo
the newly christened *Raden Ajeng*, including the
damaged wing from where the military pinnace had
collided with it, Lizet and Tamazo had apparently been
one-upping each other with their recent experiences as
pilot and navigator.

Anitra turned to Salma Youssef, sprawled on the

other lounge chair. "Heard anything from your father?" asked Anitra.

"No." Salma's tone was calm, but Anitra knew she was worried. Chief Ferrsi was fiercely dedicated to duty, and would likely stay on Polaris-G to the bitter end. He'd sent all his children and extended family away in the refugee ships. His wife and co-husband stayed because they categorically refused to leave him. Anitra assumed stubbornness ran in the family. The only thing keeping Salma on Sivari Intalo was her solemn promise to her father not to return. "The rest of us have checked in, except Uncle Omar and his family. We think he might have gone to the main jump point."

"I'm sorry to hear that." The military and the CPS had initially refused all media requests for information about any events on or off Pol-G, but rising rumors had recently forced them to issue vociferous denials. It wouldn't last. Anitra was glad that Pol-G's people had spread far and wide. Even the CPS would be hard-pressed to find and silence a hundred thousand people, each with a similar story about innocent civilian ships being destroyed at a secret blockade.

"Me, too. They were good people." She looked at her police-style wrist gauntlet. "Fifteen minutes!" she shouted toward the nav pod. She smiled at Anitra. "If I don't give them a time limit, they'll be there all day, and we need to get back to the hostel."

"Once they have a real home, what's next for you?" Salma had agreed to chaperone the underage Lizet and even more underage Tamazo while their great-grandfathers found a place for them, the kids, and the pets to live. Anitra privately hoped it would take Lizet's disapproving, stifling parents a long time to come get her.

Salma shrugged and shook her head. "Short-term private enforcement gigs, until everyone is free. Then we'll decide as a family."

Anitra couldn't imagine what it would be like to have a family that looked out for each other and made group decisions. Her parents had seemed happy to hand her over to the CPS Academy and never look back. She'd been born to save their relationship, and instead had shattered it. By the time she graduated and accepted the CPS job, they'd each had new families that didn't have room for her. She'd made her own family with friends and co-workers, or so she'd thought, until she discovered their lies. She planned to do her level best to create a new family with Gavril.

Salma sat up and leaned forward. "When are you leaving?"

"Soon, I think. The melee at the spaceport is finally getting sorted, and the Norika Deo identity I borrowed from the Pol-G census records won't hold up to an authentication check. Dalgono is the type to keep that detain-and-restrain order on me open, out of spite." Not to mention, the Sivari Intalo CPS had belatedly sent in Minder Corps personnel to help with the refugee crisis, and she wanted to be long gone by the time they got around to her.

Salma made a rude sound. "I can't believe Dalgono convinced the Aetheres investigators his attempt to steal our cargo was all a big misunderstanding."

"Sucks flux, doesn't it? But at least he's stuck on a

dying planet for a while longer, until the blockade is officially lifted." She picked up her empty cup. "Oh, sorry, the eight-month quarantine that never happened."

"Angels of chaos, but I hate politics." Salma blew out a sigh. "I'll bet the settlement company gets away with their bullshit, too."

"Probably. Settlement companies are a protected business class because the government needs them to keep the expansion going." Anitra smiled. "Oh, I meant to tell you, the Pol-G Refugee Trust is open for business—the lawyers registered it at Concordance Prime yesterday. The settlement company won't be able to touch one decimal of it. Gavril transferred ownership of the *Diam*... uh, the *Raden Ajeng* and all its contents to it this morning. The trustees can sell it or operate it as a freighter, whatever works best."

After the passengers had voted on the ship's new name, Gavril and Lizet had changed its registration IDs and put the ship in his trading company's name, to make its records neat and clean.

"Send me the details, and I'll forward them to my father on the family secure net. He's probably the only one who knows where the rest of your cargo went."

Anitra took her cup to the counter of Gavril's well-appointed kitchen... er, galley. She had a lot to learn about Gavril's trading business, starting with the correct names for things on ships. "Check your incoming. I already did."

"Oh, sorry. My cousins flood my queue daily." She worked a few seconds on her police-style gauntlet percomp. "Done."

THAT EVENING, she and Gavril finalized their itinerary for the coming few months. The ship's office was too small for two people, so they used percomps and a shipcomp display on the antique dining table. She might have been more tempted to jet away with him two years ago if he'd shown her his spacious and well-appointed ship back then.

The *Corviniana*'s living space was larger than she'd imagined, easily five times the area equivalent of her high-rise apartment on Pol-G, and had modular walls that made reconfiguration easy. He'd insisted on creating a large, high-ceilinged art studio for her, and she'd accepted. She'd had to leave all her artwork behind, since it wouldn't fit in her recycling tub of worldly goods. She needed the physical act of painting and sculpture to keep focused, or her creative little brain would pull her in a hundred different directions, and nothing would ever get done.

He'd spent the last ten days contacting customers and arranging transport orders from businesses across Sivari Intalo to fill the *Corviniana*'s cargo holds. Since she couldn't afford to be seen at the spaceport, especially once the CPS showed up, she'd holed up in the ship and put her management skills to good use inventorying cargo holds and supplies, and tracking down the best places to buy replacements. Anonymous cashflow chips, she'd discovered, had extra value on frontier planets because the settlement company couldn't track them or take a percentage of the transaction. She used some of hers to get deals and discounts on food, fuel, and art supplies. Plus printer substrates for the two new parts printers that she'd found a way to transfer from the freighter into Gavril's machine shop, as small recompense for the risks he'd taken for the refugees.

Gavril pointed to the display of their schedule. "We've got two free weeks between the delivery on Onaksat and the pickup at Asudel Station. Anyplace you've always wanted to go?" He slid his chair closer and threaded his fingers into hers. She dropped her shields to enjoy the emotional pulse of love and satisfaction he sent her way.

"Let me think about it. I mostly lived on military bases in my former career. I used to travel a lot, but I was always seeing cities and people at their worst." She raised their joined hands and kissed his thumb. "Right now, I'm enjoying nesting here with you."

He smiled. "Sinjin and Maruk want to give us two of Chaos Seven's kittens, when they're old enough, as a gift for us helping their family get off Pol-G."

She raised her eyebrows. "That's a handsome offer, considering what purebred, champion canlynxes are worth." She squeezed his fingers. She knew essential things about him, like that he was a good person with a generous heart, but she knew very little about his day-to-day life. She looked forward to finding out. "Do you even like cats?"

"Yes. I inherited my mother's old cat, Lopar. He lived to almost thirty, and I still miss him." He shrugged almost apologetically. "I didn't have a reason to find another one until I met you."

She laughed. "Your mother named her cat 'Lopar'?

He must have been one of those reckless kittens, always getting into mischief and proud of it."

He chuckled. "I think she named him after my father, to be perfectly honest. By the time I got him, Lopar was sedate and lazy." He cast a glance at the kitchen and smiled. "We'll have to do kitten-proofing for all the cabinets."

"Not to mention my studio, or we'll have paw-shaped paint tracks everywhere." She loved the idea of having cats, and shared her pleasure with him. She reached across and caught a couple of his turquoise-colored braids in her fingers. "Your hair is very sexy, but these will be irresistible to kittens." She pulled him in for a kiss. "It certainly is to me."

He pulled her onto his padded chair so she sat on his knees, facing him. He kissed her slowly, sensuously, as if they had all the time in the galaxy. She pushed his loose tunic open so she could feel his bare skin. His hand slid under the hem of her shirt toward her breast. She held her breath in delicious anticipation of his touch.

He pulled her close for another kiss, and she felt his waves of love twine with hers. "I want a family with you, so if that includes kittens, I'll take that trade."

# EPILOGUE

---

Ivar Okeanos sat straight and still in his auditorium seat as the CGC High Command Space Division military tribunal announced their findings from their investigation of the events in the Polaris-Gamma system. The tribunal's speaker, a woman with iron-gray short hair and perfect Standard English diction, had started twenty minutes ago on the minor infractions and had saved the serious charges for the end.

"In the matter of CPS Security Officer Paderau's unilateral order to deploy *Bassilon*'s pinnaces to deter the civilian *Deset Diamantov* from jumping at the Polaris-Zeta jump point, the tribunal finds the order within regulation, as *Bassilon* was not in combat at the time. There is no evidence the freighter used any weapons, or even had any to use. Considering the loss of the pinnace, however, the tribunal finds the order recklessly endangered both military personnel and the non-combatant freighter. This finding will be entered in Security Officer Paderau's profile."

Ivar flicked a glance at Paderau, one row up and four places to the right. Like most CPS personnel assigned to Space Div, she didn't bother with military protocol, and was slouching in her chair with a frown. She ought to be smiling, because she'd gotten off easy. The injured pilot had survived the accident because the freighter's captain shared their sensor data with the pinnaces that had been attacking at Paderau's order.

"In the matter of CPS Security Officer Shailun's unilateral order to the entire task force to open fire on civilian ships at the Polaris-Gamma jump point, the tribunal finds the order in violation, as the task force was in combat at the time. As such, the captains of the other ships who did not open fire are not in violation of a lawful command."

Murmuring arose. The speaker sipped water until it subsided. Ivar imagined twelve captains heaved a sigh of relief.

"In the matter of Security Officer Shailun's detaining and restraining Commodore Britton and her executive staff on the flagship to prevent them from countermanding the fire orders, the tribunal finds the action a flagrant violation of regulation, and in direct opposition to keeping the galactic peace. The tribunal denies the CPS's requests for parole and remand. Security Officer Shailun will remain in High Command custody until sentencing."

That was unexpected. That supercilious,

mastermind-wannabe deserved everything he got, but Ivar suspected he was being scapegoated to protect the regular military and CPS security officers on the other blockade frigates who had acted on Shailun's order, with or without the consent of their captains.

Sure enough, the tribunal found the other security officers had acted within regulation based on the best information they had at the time. They wouldn't even get the negative incident flag in their profile that Paderau's now had. He'd seen it happen too many times in his twenty-two years in the various CGC military divisions to even be surprised. Besides, Nieth Sobek had predicted as much.

Finally, the speaker got to the findings that had kept him up at night for the last three months.

"In the matter of the charges by the Citizen Protection Service that frigate captains Chesterton and Okeanos at the Polaris-Zeta jump point refused a command order to use lethal force if necessary to stop civilian ships from leaving the system, the tribunal finds the captains not guilty. The order to fire on private and commercial ships did not come from the commodore; the rules of engagement did." The speaker looked up from her tablet, and the written words paused in the overhead display. She swept the audience with her gaze. "As a side note, the tribunal has opened a separate enquiry into the events that precipitated the blockade in the first place. During our investigation, evidence came to light that merits further investigation."

A whispering wave of voices washed through the auditorium. Paderau's frown deepened. Ivar suspected the "health quarantine" excuse wouldn't stand up to close scrutiny, meaning both the CPS and Space Div were going to be engaging in major ass-covering in the near future. When they did, he hoped they'd throw the greedy, callous settlement company off the sky skimmer to lighten the load.

The speaker once again read from her tablet. "In the matter of charges by the CPS that Chesterton and Okeanos purposefully provided information to the Polaris-Gamma government regarding the existence of the Zeta jump point so their people could break quarantine, and that Okeanos knowingly provided a flawed, exploitable navigation solution to the Zeta blockade, the tribunal finds both charges completely frivolous and without merit. The promulgation of current, accurate stellar navigation data is a core mission of the Space Division."

Once again, the speaker looked up. "We are not in the business of falsifying, manipulating, or withholding such information from citizens. We are not the Central League. We are the Central Galactic Concordance, and we will behave accordingly." Her frosty tone and precise articulation should have driven the point home, though Ivar doubted the CPS thought it applied to them. "The tribunal hereby denies the CPS's request to order Captain Okeanos or any of his staff to submit to a telepathic interrogation to determine his motives and actions regarding the Polaris system incidents. No other evidence suggests Okeanos acted improperly; subjective suspicion is an insufficient justification."

For the benefit of Paderau and whoever else was

watching, Ivar kept his face still, as if he'd expected to be exonerated all along. As the Polaris events proved, the CPS considered their agenda more important than justice or the rule of law. The interrogation would have cratered Ivar's career and Sobek's. He wasn't a minder, and had no defenses against a telepath. Sobek had more secrets than just colluding with him to avert a massacre. As it was, fifty-three civilian ships had been damaged beyond repair, and nearly two hundred lives had been lost, including one spacer who'd been trying to rescue a doomed escape pod. The skirmish had been very far from one of Space Div's shining moments.

The speaker closed her tablet, and the auditorium displays faded to nothing. "The proceedings of this tribunal are concluded. I will once again remind you that *none* of the information from the investigation reports or tribunal findings is to be disclosed outside this room, or discussed, characterized, or alluded to with anyone, in person or in writing, or in any digital or virtual form." She stood. "This tribunal is closed." She stepped off the dais and left the room.

Commodore Britton, seated in the front row, stood and turned to face the audience. Her expression was unreadable, but the stiffness of her posture evinced tension. "Dismissed."

Ivar waited until others around him started to stand before he stood up himself. Out of the corner of his eye, he noted Paderau's contemptuous, suspicious glare directed toward him, then toward Sobek, seated on the other side of the auditorium.

Ivar ignored it. Sobek had already nudged

Commodore Britton's second-in-command, Yount, about the importance of having trustworthy, competent people around. Yount would mention it to Britton, and the odds were good that she'd request all new security officers for her task force. Space Div would likely be happy to accommodate her request, since the CPS security officers had come within a nanometer of outright mutiny. Paderau would have to find a new obsession.

When he got to the aisle stairs that led up to the exit, he found himself walking next to Commander Cristhian, one of Britton's strategy officers. Sobek suggested he treat them all with respect, and listen carefully when they spoke. Forecasters as a group more often than not canceled each other out. If they agreed on a single agenda, however, they could be very effective in getting what they wanted. The trick was to figure out what that was.

"Captain Okeanos." Cristhian's expression and tone reflected delighted surprise. "I hear you're being considered for a bigger ship." Regular body shop visits obviously kept the man looking youthfully athletic, but Ivar knew he'd been in Space Division nearly as long as Sobek had. Thanks to modern medicine and sophisticated body-makeover techniques, few people looked their age these days, but when the time came, Ivar doubted he'd elect such a deliberately young-and-earnest look.

"I go where Space Div sends me," Ivar replied noncommittally.

"Would Sobek go with you? The commodore's flagship will soon have an opening. Captain Ap Llew put in for a transfer."

Ah, the ostensible point of the conversation. "I hadn't heard that."

Cristhian gave him a blinding smile. "Just this morning."

"Ah, well then," Ivar said.

They reached the top of the stairs and passed through the wide exit arch. He snapped his fingers. "Damn, I forgot my umbrella." He turned quickly and headed back down into the auditorium before Cristhian could come up with an excuse to go with him.

At his row, he sidestepped past the seats until he found his, then crouched to find the closed umbrella right where he'd deliberately left it. He stood and slid it into the long pocket of his black-and-chrome uniform overcoat, then sidestepped forward to the other set of aisle stairs, which were less crowded, hiding his smile as he did so. Cristhian might be on the Commodore's vaunted strategy team, but he was a lousy personal strategist.

Ivar made his way through the lobby out onto the clear glass walkway that fronted the building. The capital of the entire galactic government had an official name, but everyone called it the City of Spires. Two hundred years before, the new Central Galactic Concordance government had been flush with funds they'd recovered from the Central League, the acquisitive, murderous, deeply corrupt previous regime. The CGC went on a spending spree, building a galaxy-class interstellar fleet for keeping the peace and commissioning a fantastic showcase city of gleaming glass that reached for the sky, built on the rubble of the Central League's final demise.

Outside, a light misting rain mixed with hazy

sunshine. He pulled out his umbrella and powered it up with shade setting, then inserted himself in a crowd of tourists and let them carry him along to the nearest public transportation platform's kiosk. His precautions were probably overkill, but Cristhian's calculated approach meant he was still under scrutiny.

He ordered a secure solo autocab, then waited for it to go airborne before giving it the coordinates of the military-approved restaurant where he and Sobek had agreed to meet after the tribunal, assuming it went as they'd hoped. Justice, as the displaced settlers already knew, was sometimes hard to come by. When the current newstrends finally flatlined, he planned to find a way to let the settlers know as much of the truth as possible.

When he arrived at the restaurant, he discovered Sobek was already there and had arranged a secure booth, as protocol dictated for senior officers still under the restricted operating procedures of a covert operations task force.

They ordered and paid for a full meal and no-kick drinks. As soon as the silverware and drinks arrived, he reported the conversation he'd had with Cristhian, word for word.

After a long moment, she appeared to come to a decision.

"You need a new second-in-command."

He'd been both dreading and expecting this day for the last two years. "May I know the reason?"

"I've become a liability. Retirement is my best way out. Britton's strategy team suspects what I am—took them long enough—and wants to use you to get closer to me. Once they do, they'll have leverage over you for protecting me."

He gave her a small smile. "Wouldn't they be surprised to learn you've been protecting me." He didn't phrase it as a question.

Her eyebrows raised slightly. "And why would I do that?"

He considered his answer. In the nine years they'd known each other, they'd never discussed their unlikely partnership so directly. They might never have the opportunity again. "You think I'll be a catalyst in something important to you."

It was his best working theory for why Sobek, with nearly eighty years of Space Div experience, had aligned her star chart with his for nine years instead of retiring as she'd been planning at the time. She'd taught him how to swim in shark-infested waters of the powerful, tradition-bound, political military. She'd also trusted him with the secret that she was a minder forecaster, asserting that he'd figure it out sooner rather than later.

"A wild card, perhaps." She took a sip of her blue fizzy. "Forecaster talent doesn't work like that ridiculous potboiler serial, where the main characters place bets on space races or commodity markets when they needs funds. It's more like watching the flux sensors in transit. The individual waves and currents are impossible to predict, but the combined result moves the ship in a predictable direction." She unfolded her napkin and refolded it into a shape that resembled a boat. "I wouldn't be a good fit for the strategy team. They're dedicated to self-preservation and the status quo. My talent has been telling me for years that change is coming and we're headed for trouble. We, as in, the whole Concordance."

He knew better than to ask her what she meant, because she'd turn it around to a question and twist him in philosophical knots. He wasn't a forecaster, but given enough time, he could sometimes see the patterns when she gave him a hint.

Their food arrived, and the conversation turned to lighter subjects for the rest of the meal.

Ivar poured each of them more water from the table carafe. "Any recommendations on your successor?"

"No," she said. "Your instincts are much better than mine about people. Do whatever you did to find me."

He suspected she'd actually found him, and helped Space Div along in getting her name and record on the candidate list. He'd selected her because she hadn't blown flux up his butt about his illustrious family or looked down on his less-than-illustrious résumé, and her Space Div experience filled a knowledge gap on his part.

"It's been an honor to serve with you, Nieth." He touched his chest in the sketch of a salute. "I'll miss you like hell."

"I'll miss you, too." She knocked back the last of her fizzy drink like it was a hard shot. "Won't miss much else about the military, though. It's not the organization I enlisted in anymore. I also won't miss moving to a new home base every other year, and never getting to see my family."

Ivar smiled. "You must have seen your husband a few times, at least, or you wouldn't have four great kids."

She laughed. "Okay, yeah, you're right. But I jetted in

and out of their lives too often, and I want to spoil my grandchildren and great-grandchildren to make up for it." She folded her napkin flat next to her empty plate. "You should find someone to be in love with. When trouble comes, you need that someone to have your back, to remind you what you're sacrificing for."

"Yes, sir." He smiled, amused. "You'll be an excellent grandparent. Your kids don't know what they're in for."

She chuckled. "Come on, let's go back to the ship and set the cleaning bots after Paderau's spy eyes. She needs something to keep her occupied until Britton transfers her." She gave him a pointed look. "Meanwhile, you should find a 'bigger ship' for yourself, away from the strategy group."

He laughed and saluted. "Yes, sir. Right away, sir. Consider it done!"

## ABOUT THE BOOK

Thanks for reading *Last Ship Off Polaris-G*. If you want more space opera, adventure, and romance, check out the next book in the Central Galactic Concordance series, OVERLOAD FLUX. Two misfits have secrets they must keep. But if they expose the secrets of a corrupt pharma corp, they may end up dead.

*Last Ship Off Polaris-G* introduces challenges that minders face in this far future universe. It also introduces a character or two who you'll see in coming books. I hope you'll come along for the ride.

\*

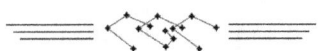

**When the cure for a deadly disease is stolen, two misfits are all that stands between greed and intergalactic tragedy.**

Luka Foxe can't let anyone know about his secret mental abilities. Debilitated by their influence when faced with violence, the brilliant forensic investigator now only takes assignments involving theft. But when he has to hunt down a hijacked vaccine for a galaxy-wide pandemic, the tragic first clue is his best friend's brutal murder.

Nightshift guard Mairwen Morganthur knows she must keep a low profile. The product of illegal genetic alteration, she's a lethal weapon with no social graces. But when she's tasked to protect a detective with frightening intuition, she finds herself falling for him even though he could expose her.

Racing to recover the cure for a galaxy-wide pandemic, Luka is surprised by his developing feelings for the capable-but-mysterious guard. And Mairwen may have to risk everything by revealing her identity, with deadly mercenaries hot on their tail.

Can the unlikely pair survive an interplanetary conspiracy long enough to save lives and find love?

*Overload Flux* is the first novel in the sweeping Central Galactic Concordance space opera series. If you like haunted characters, compelling mysteries, and interstellar romance, then you'll enjoy Carol Van Natta's epic tale.

**Buy Overload Flux to uncover
cosmic corruption today!**

*Author.CarolVanNatta.com/OF*

\*

# ABOUT THE AUTHOR

Carol Van Natta is a USA TODAY bestselling science fiction and fantasy author. Works include the award-winning Central Galactic Concordance space opera series and the Ice Age Shifters® paranormal romance series. In addition, she edits the Pets in Space science fiction romance anthology.

She shares her Colorado home with just the right number of eccentric cats. Connect with her on the web at Author.CarolVanNatta.com.

\*